Praise for Deborah Blumenthal's debut novel, *Fat Chance*

WITHDRAWN

"Food and men are two of Maggie O'Leary's favorite pastimes.... To snag her star, she ignores her own antidieting dictates and sheds the pounds but eventually finds that you can get a man and eat your cake, too."
—*People*

"Light as a cupcake and as fun to devour, Blumenthal's debut novel will likely find many fans."
—*Booklist*

"Deborah Blumenthal's deliciously amusing novel offers a refreshing chick-lit twist: a heroine who embraces with gusto her inner—and generously proportioned outer— food-loving self. Zaftig Maggie O'Leary happily devours barbecued ribs rather than obsessing about whether her own will be visible to the naked eye—and builds a high-p

the

f

—

What Men Want

Deborah Blumenthal

**RED
DRESS
I N K**
™

WHAT MEN WANT

A Red Dress Ink novel

ISBN 0-373-89569-0

© 2006 by Deborah Blumenthal.

www.RedDressInk.com

Printed in U.S.A.

To Ralph

Chapter One

There are men that you meet and forget. And then there are men who keep you up at night...like Slaid Warren.

It's not what you're thinking. Yes, the newspaper photo made him look like a runway model with his deep-set brooding eyes and long dark bangs swept back off his forehead. But that was all beside the point.

Slaid worked for one major New York City newspaper, and I worked for another. So the thrusting and parrying between us was professional, all business, and it took place in print and on the phone, not between the sheets—not those sheets, anyway. We weren't lovers. We weren't friends. In fact, we had never even met.

So, you know that I would have done whatever it took to scoop him, not only to get ahead professionally and win kudos from my colleagues, but also to enjoy the end-of-the-day phone call that inevitably followed slighting my success, thus convincing me of my triumph. It was usually brief, just a couple of sentences. But in those few seconds, I chalked up the fact that I had him in a headlock and it wasn't where he liked to be.

"You missed the story," he said dismissively in one of our early conversations just months after I had been given the column. Of course he started the conversation without bowing to convention and introducing himself. Unthinkable to *him* that someone couldn't recognize his voice, and anyway, we had an ongoing dialogue, interrupted just to allow for new columns to appear.

"If it helps you to deal with it," I said, leaning back in my chair and warming to his discomfort with the realization that my column had left him in the dust. He laughed heartily as though acknowledging a good joke.

"No, babe," he said, abruptly cutting off the laughter like a motorboat engine suddenly out of power. "Dealing is not the point. I was out nailing the *real* story. Your column was filler." Before I could respond, he hung up.

To backtrack, Slaid Warren and I both covered city politics. "Slaid in the City" was his column. He had me there. How could I hope to top that? Through no effort of his own, he had the good fortune to be born to parents hip enough to give him a cool, albeit weird, name. The only damage I could inflict was to write him e-mails spelling it S-L-A-Y-E-D, in keeping with that of readers who disagreed with him.

My column, I'm loath to admit, had an agonizingly mundane name, echoing a sparrow chirping: "Street Beat." Nothing there to summon the grit and substance of a tough investigative column. Then there was my vanilla name: Jenny George. As one well-intentioned boyfriend once commented, "It sounds more like the name of a cheerleader or talk-show host than a serious reporter. Why don't you just change it?"

Just change it? Although there are more things about me that I would change than not, my name isn't one of them. And while a name that was heftier or more commanding—Lana Davis Harriman or Katherine Clotilde Porter III, for example—might have drawn me into public prominence faster, I love and respect my parents—imperfect as they showed themselves to be when naming their children. (Can you imagine Burt as a name for my older brother? If they had a second son, would he have been Ernie?) Anyway, it was the name they gave me and it seemed almost sacrilegious to consider changing it. Whatever.

As for the column, it had been called "Street Beat" for years, it was well read, and as my editors saw it, why mess with success? To their credit though, they weren't interested in redesigning the paper and coming up with younger, hipper column heads like, "Thing," or "What I Was Thinking," that other papers presumably thought would attract younger readers because they sounded edgier. The paper was secure in its identity and fortunately it had even advanced to the point of covering music written after the "Blue Danube Waltz."

I had put in ten years at the *New York Daily* before taking over the column, starting as a secretary—not an assistant, the term used more often these days—right after college. Since I showed outstanding capability in juggling the phones and discreetly giving everyone the proper messages so that their colleagues didn't find out that headhunters were returning their calls, or worse, places like AA, I was asked to stay on after my six-month probation, sparing me the humiliation of circling ads in the *Times* and calling people in human resources, a name that made me think of organ banks.

I was promoted to editorial assistant, and finally cub reporter, which meant that I earned the right to go downtown to cover a press conference by the Consumer Product Safety Commission on lawnmower safety (never mind that as an apartment dweller I had never even seen one) and up to Connecticut to report on a factory that made walking sticks. I had my shorthand to thank—or blame—plus my trusty tape recorder and my reputation for staying with a story until every source was questioned practically to death. I'm not sure if that's because I'm tenacious about ferreting out the truth, or that I'm so insecure that I overresearch. Let's just say that I took the old journalism adage to heart—"If your mother says she loves you, check it out."

The column was actually something of a gift following a tense investigation of a shelter for women who were victims of domestic violence. I spent two nights in one and wrote a story exposing the failures of the system, including a lack of policing that led to boyfriends finding their way in and spending the night. Apparently the current columnist had opened the paper one morning to find an obit of a colleague who died at age fifty of a massive heart attack and immediately submitted his resignation so that he could spend more time with his family. But ultimately the decisive factor that led to my becoming a columnist with all the power that comes with it might well have been the fact that the stars were in proper alignment.

In any case, it was a prized, if competitive, job. It was a bit daunting, at first, to find myself up against some ace metro reporters, including Slaid, who had a far wider net of contacts than I did and far more experience. Being male didn't hurt him either, plus he was slick at taking advantage of the buddy network built up through jobs at various papers and magazines, so that disgruntled insiders seemed to gravitate to him. Then once he sat down with them, he was one of the guys and always on their side, at least until he was in front of the computer screen and the story came out.

And how was I viewed? Think perky former cheerleader. In fact, I was told on my thirtieth birthday that I had the cherubic face and fawning grin of an eighteen-year-old Goldie Hawn. Not a bad thing, but needless to say, with only one year now on the job, I had a lot of catching up to do to earn credibility and authenticity.

But back to Slaid. Be assured that I would never denigrate a colleague needlessly. He was known to be trustworthy to a fault, at least judging from the fact that months back he had spent a few weeks locked up in prison for refusing to turn over his notes after he interviewed a mafia don following the murder of a member of a rival family. It led to a juicy column and his refusal to cooperate with a police investigation on the grounds that New York's shield laws protected journalists from turning over their notes and revealing their sources.

I don't believe for a minute that Slaid withheld his notes—as some of my more mean-spirited colleagues have flippantly suggested—because he knew he could count on his buddies from the six o'clock news to make a show of hanging out supportively at the prison 24/7, guaranteeing that his popularity would soar, not to mention bringing him hearty fare like pasta alfredo and osso bucco from Little Italy so that he would be spared the ordeal of subsisting on prison food. That wasn't such a really big deal. After all, he didn't get to drink the Pinot Grigio or the Barolo. They were confiscated; I know that for a fact.

But watching him on TV, I realized that he one-upped me in another, more fundamental way. As he was interviewed coming out of prison (and the hype! You'd think he'd served twenty years and a wrongful conviction was overturned), he stops and turns to stare directly into the camera's eye, speaking softly, in a controlled, almost wounded kind of way—like an Italian film star in a noirish setting. No one could miss the fact that his deep-set eyes and shadow of a beard, combined with the upturned collar on his worn sport jacket, gave him that soulful bedroom look that I know he was going for. And what did he say? Would you believe he quoted James Madison? "'Popular government without popular information or the means of acquiring it is but a prologue to a farce or a tragedy.'"

Bravura performance. The erudition coupled with the intensity of his look. Little me, on the other hand, would try and fail at impersonating the lost, waifish air of a Daryl Hannah type. Instead, I'd look vulnerable and helpless. Instead of alerting viewers to the fact that my incarceration was part of a distressing new pattern of attack on the freedom of the press, I would merely look distraught as though I was weathering the flu. I'd undoubtedly say something rambling and incoherent because I hadn't slept well due to the hard beds and thin mattresses, the claustrophobic sizes of the cells and the over-crowded conditions. My hair would be twirled up in a ponytail so that it didn't droop like seaweed be-cause of the absence of Aveda Sap Moss shampoo or Kiehl's Silk Groom (do they let you take those things to jail?)—my lifelines to vibrant hair. And without Nars Orgasm blush and Chanel lip gloss, I'd look merely washed out, not sultry columnist wronged by the system.

So instead of *reporting it,* Slaid Warren *was* the news for a good week after that, and as I learned, spending time in the big house, especially for hold-ing such high moral values, can really up your In-ternet-chatter quotient, not to mention boosting future book advances. If I didn't know better, I would have guessed that Slaid had arranged it, maybe even sleeping with the judge (who was divorced and not half-bad-looking, even in her muumuu-size black robe) to set the whole thing up.

But these days, praise the Lord, Slaid was out, a free man—free to take himself to movie premiers and hang out at all-night celebrity-backed restaurant openings that were destined to be covered in the next day's papers where he was photographed snuggling one fetching model or another and generally cavort-ing with the A-list.

And while we had very different types of social lives and went our separate ways, we both seemed to have similar instincts when it came to sniffing out a good story, leading to columns that were often breaking the same news.

The problem was we were more than just rivals *in our columns;* we had become rivals *in our lives,* elevating one-upmanship to a spectator sport for readers, not to mention the sword sharpening that went on privately between us, on the phone.

What do I mean?

When I wrote about the mayor using workers under city contract to renovate playgrounds to work in his Fifth Avenue town house, Slaid had a similar column as I guessed he would. So I was lucky enough to know someone who worked for the construction company. I topped him by offering obscure details about the particular style of moldings that the mayor was installing (egg and dart) and added another juicy detail—he had them working overtime so they could finish the job in time for his annual Christmas bash. (Catered by a company headed by a friend of a friend. I held off describing the canapés that he ordered, baja ceviche, crab rangoon and caviar d'aubergine, among others, and the cranberry Stoli martinis, juicy details to foodies, but really a bit beside the point.) That phone call was a memorable one too.

"Egg and dart?"

I didn't say anything.

"What the hell is egg and dart?"

"Ask one of your interior-design sources," I said.

"Why would I know people like that?"

"Aren't you gay?" I asked, expertly choking back the laughter welling up in my throat.

"Fuck," he said, hanging up.

Then there was the column I wrote about a writer at Slaid's paper who was caught fabricating a news source in a story that he covered without ever going to the scene. Story after story ensued as if the paper was so guilt-ridden that it felt it had to purge itself repeatedly, in print.

I ended my column:

News about newsmakers is replacing the real news, inadvertently turning liars and cheats into media stars and future authors of tell-all books. Can't TV-news types find more reputable people to interview? Can't Slaid Warren drop his long columns about soul-searching over lunch at Vong and instead find someone gifted, talented or at least more illuminating to lunch with for his column? It's time to leave the fate of bad journalists to the editors and publishers who hired them and move on to the real news.

"So why didn't *you* write about *your* lunch with heads of state instead of wasting trees to write about *my* column?" he said, putting me on the spot.

"You're too sensitive," I said, yawning. "Didn't your mother ever tell you not to take things so to heart?"

"It happens to be a major scandal among serious journalists. I guess that fact passed you by."

"I got it," I said, "about eight million words ago. Give it up."

"Sweetheart," he said, getting to his famous exit line. "I didn't get where I am by giving up." He hung up and there I was holding the phone once again after the line went dead. I pressed redial and he picked up on the first ring.

"Slaid?"

"Yeah."

"Just one more thing," I said. Then *I* hung up.

Chapter Two

It was several weeks before Christmas and I left the office early to buy presents. There were no time clocks to punch. As long as my columns were in on time, my hours were my own. Unfortunately, that meant that I usually worked myself harder than any boss would have dared. News didn't stop for weekends or holidays, and neither did I. Almost any time of day or night, I might hear the first bars of "A Little Night Music," my cell's ring *du jour*. If I could have figured how to do it, I would have used "A Hard Day's Night" or "Working on a Chain Gang."

Every year I vowed to start squirreling away gifts in August, so that by December first I'd have the whole heap of them wrapped up all pretty and ready and I'd be spared any and all anxiety of what to buy and where to go. But that happens in the closets of

meticulous homemakers who take pleasure in offering gifts of homemade flavored vinegars in antique
bottles bearing scalloped labels hand printed in olive-
colored ink, following instructions they've clipped
from the perfect holiday pages of *House & Garden* or
Real Simple.

It had been a year now that Chris and I had been
living together. Since I had a one-bedroom apartment when we met and he had a two-, I moved in
with him, a definite step up, so to speak from my
small walk-up on the Upper East Side with no view
to speak of.

Chris's apartment was open, airy and contemporary, a mix of Mies, Ikea and Craig's List. It was in
Kips Bay, a modern high-rise complex in the East 30s
designed by I. M. Pei with floor-to-ceiling picture
windows and exterior walls of exposed concrete that
gave it a spare, contemporary look, even though it
was built decades back.

Things between us were good and I wanted to get
Chris a serious present. Unfortunately, I hadn't put
in the time sleuthing through his closet to check his
size or to figure out what he needed. Yes, I should
have known, but for some reason I couldn't keep the
numbers in my head and remember whether he was
a 32 or 34 waist, or a 16 shirt collar or 16-1/2. And
then there was the question of what a medium trans-
lated to or whether a shirt or sweater should be
bought in a large.

Why was it so much easier to shop for women? Off the top of my head I could come up with twenty things that would be perfect gifts for me: a cashmere scarf, a cashmere bathrobe, a pashmina wrap, a great silk nightgown, gold, anything gold, better yet platinum, a fabulous Marc Jacobs handbag, a Tod's handbag (yes, they're all a fortune, but don't put a price on my happiness), Juicy anything, sable makeup brushes, or maybe even an expensive hairbrush.

I knew that I would buy my best friend, Ellen Gaines, a cashmere camisole and matching cardigan. My mother would get a silk blouse and a new scarf, and I'd buy my father plaid flannel pajamas and a robe from his favorite Web site, L.L.Bean.

But when it came to boyfriends, it seemed as though I was stuck buying the same clichéd goodies year after year—a new lamb's-wool crewneck or a cashmere turtleneck sweater, a couple of whimsical ties from MOMA, although I really couldn't remember the last time Chris wore one, and the old fall-back staples like the latest tomes of nonfiction (or anything by Stephen Ambrose) or the Swiss Army knife with multipurpose pullout tools that could do jobs ranging from opening beer bottles to jump-starting cars.

Fortunately, Chris wasn't obsessed with material wealth. He worked in advertising and was an REI (you know, the sporty catalog) kind of guy. His hair was dirty blond and he had pale blue eyes. His wardrobe? Think of Wranglers, Frye boots, pullover sweaters, T–shirts, a beat–up leather baseball jacket and one or two preppie–looking sport jackets. I don't think that he owned a serious tie. If he ever wore ties, I wasn't around to see it. In fact, the only time I remember seeing him take a tie out of his closet was when he decided to tie my hands together one day, on a whim, after we had finished a bottle of particularly good champagne and were feeling, well, experimental.

I wanted to give him something that would remind him of me whenever he looked at it. Something that he would keep for ages that would get even better with time, like a great leather jacket. So pj's were out, which he never wore anyway, and so was a bathrobe, even though I loved the thick terry ones that were as cozy as down on a cold night. Of course, Chris never got cold, and when he did, he pulled on a hooded gray sweatshirt.

I walked the aisles of Saks, and then headed uptown to Bloomingdale's—the after-hours pastime of every red-blooded, material New York woman. I started out in the men's fragrance area sniffing one cologne after another until my nerve receptors were on overload and I was unable to tell the differences and was getting a dull headache. What was I doing? Chris didn't wear cologne anyway—hated it, he once said—still I felt I had to cover all the bases. The store was hot, crowded and overheated—big surprise—and I peeled off my coat. The truth was, Chris was Dial-soap clean and on-sale shampoo. He had a full bottle of Calvin Klein body wash that was a gift from way back that he had never even opened.

Finally, I picked out a great camel-colored leather overnight bag with lots of side pockets, which I knew that I'd probably use more than he would. It had great brass hardware, and I knew the leather would soften with age and look better the more he used it. Of course, he didn't travel much—it was always tough for him to get away from the office, especially since he worked on so many different accounts, and inevitably seemed to be on deadline.

As I stood in line to pay for the bag, it occurred to me that if Chris ever decided to leave me, he would be walking out in style, a disturbing thought. I bought it anyway, and as I was making my way out of the store, I passed a display for Calvin Klein underwear. I stopped and stared at the advertisement showing just the midsection of a very, very well-toned *Men's Health*–type cover boy. Was it retouched, or was there a real man who actually looked like that? While it was a body that every woman craved to run her hands over, it was also the body of a man who spent countless hours working on himself. After using up all that strength for self-improvement, what did men like that have left to offer women? Undoubtedly, perfection took its toll. I put the package of briefs that I had in my hand back on the rack.

When I got home, I wedged the overnight bag into the back of my closet, even though I knew that if I dropped it in the middle of the living-room floor, Chris would step over it without even realizing what it was. My timing was perfect.

"Hey," he said, coming through the door, as if on cue. How could I miss the cherry-red Saks shopping bag under his arm? Now, *that* was sweet. He had been shopping too. He wasn't one to breeze into Saks and buy himself something. He'd sit at the computer and log on to Lands' End and order whatever in blue (safe because it matched his eyes), or maybe green, yellow, on a whim. The only time he actually went shopping was when he was under the gun and just about out of shirts or sweaters, or if he found that the cuffs of his pants were frayed just before he had an appointment with a client.

I'll never forget the time that he needed a tuxedo for an awards ceremony. I took him to Macy's (a daunting outing no matter how much you needed a store that offered variety) and he had a panicked look on his face like he was visiting an alien planet. He tried on jacket after jacket and stared at himself in the mirror as though he were trying to fit himself into a space suit. Personally, I thought that he looked adorable in black-tie, but that didn't matter. After trying on the twentieth suit—I lost count—

he finally just shook as if he were having a seizure and let the jacket shimmy down his arms and drop to the floor.

"I'm not wearing one of these suckers," he said, walking off and leaving it there. I waited for a moment to see if he went back to spit on it, but instead he strode out of the store as if he had just gleefully submitted his resignation from a dead-end job. He ended up going in a plain black wool suit with a ruffled tuxedo shirt and colorful red-and-black satin bow tie with a Mickey Mouse design on it that he bought in a children's store.

But now, package in hand, I could see that at least he had made the effort and had gone to a respectable store rather than a vintage junk shop recommended by one of the twentysomething art directors that he worked with, and it thrilled me. It's not that there's anything wrong with the vintage polyester shifts in avocado-and-orange prints, or the glam o'rama sequined cardigans that you can find downtown on Broadway or in Soho. It's just that I'm not the beanpole-model type who can carry off those quirky looks and appear as though I'm wearing what's ahead on the runway for Prada. On me, they just look peculiar and "what was I thinking?"

Not that I'm a classics girl by any means. When we first met, Chris got me a bottle of Chanel No.5. Nice, traditional, but I had never worn it and never would. Everyone's supposed to love the fragrance, of course, but to me it smells off, like something musty that you find on a dusty dressing table when you're cleaning out the apartment of your dead grand-mother. (He couldn't have known that I was an Yves Saint Laurent fan—he was a copywriter not a nose.) Obviously, he had been taken under the wing of a saleswoman who saw his vulnerability and promised him, "You can't go wrong with a classic scent."

"So," I said, looking at everything but the bag. "How was work?"

"Okay," he said in a distant voice, like a child who hasn't decompressed yet after coming home from school. Chris worked for a top Madison Avenue ad agency, a job that was as cool as a real job could be. Most of the employees shlumped around in jeans, T-shirts and carpenter's overalls. The rare occasions when guys showed up in a suit and tie brought the expected droll comment from passersby:

"Job interview?"

Invariably, the answer was a small, somber shake of the head and then the barely audible utterance "fu-neral," even though it was rarely, if ever, the case.

Chris's office resembled a teenager's bedroom or something out of the Pottery Barn Teens catalog, with orange blow-up chairs, a white fluffy woolen rug, a boom box where he played his favorite CDs all day and a blue denim couch where he took naps or just stretched his legs to increase blood flow to the brain to boost creativity, or at least consciousness.

Some copywriters and art directors even used their offices as if they were their primary residences, especially after divorces, when it was no surprise to see someone walking in with a blanket and pillow under their arm. It was that laid-back.

Even though Chris didn't shop much, he enjoyed coming with me to stores like Urban Outfitters where I always picked up whimsical versions of ordinary T-shirts and denim skirts, and he bought kitschy things for his office like copies of old-fashioned metal lunch boxes, a Venus-flytrap coin bank and a plastic-and-chrome clock that looked as if it belonged in a fifties-style diner.

Did I mention the teen-room design made sense because Chris had just turned thirty-two, (although he looked twenty-one) and he was almost four years younger than I am? Whatever.

Anyway, there was almost a carnival atmosphere at the agency most of the time—except when a client would call to say that there was a change in the marketing calendar because the CEO had to fly to London, and they needed to see a new campaign in two weeks instead of two months. Then laid-back employees snapped to, turning into frantic martinets who invariably came up with something brilliant to save their asses and careers.

"We got a new account," Chris said, dropping his overstuffed army-green military-surplus backpack in the middle of the living room. He kicked off his boots and stretched his legs out on our new white duck Pottery Barn couch with the down-wrapped cushions. It replaced the couch shrouded in black cotton that Chris had found on Craig's List offered for free to anyone who would pick it up in Staten Island.

Our new couch was the first piece of furniture that we bought together, not counting the cheapo coffee table from West Elm. Eventually, we hoped to buy chairs and decent lamps to go with the couch.

I raised my eyebrows.

"A liquid diet," he said, unenthused.

"*Another* one?"

He closed his eyes and nodded.

"What's it called?"

"That's my job," he said, frowning. "The client was toying with 'skinny shake,' but when they proposed it, the conference room went silent so they gave me a week to come up with something to make it fly."

I screwed up my face. Would clones of Metrecal, the meal-in-a-can diet drink that my mother tried long ago, be reborn again and again? I remembered the commercials showing the likely candidates for the drink—two girls walking along a beach wearing sweatshirts to cover up their chubby bodies.

A new generation of suckers is born every minute, I guess, and that was what Madison Avenue banked on. It always amazed me that Chris made twice the money that I did by coming up with ways of selling products that nobody needed but every-body bought because they were convinced that they did, at least until something new came along to take its place.

"Striptease," I said.

"Striptease," he repeated, bobbing his head from left to right like a wooden doll with a spring-loaded head. Knowing Chris, it would take him a while to rule on it. "Striptease." Still bobbing. He shook his head finally.

"Wouldn't work for Middle America."

"Wanna eat out?" I said, changing the subject.

"Whatever," he said, shrugging. "Oh, Moose is in town," he said, coming over and briefly nuzzling my neck before going over to the refrigerator. Moose was his college roommate. "Maybe we should set up a dinner." I nodded.

I think the reason that Chris and I stayed together for going on a year now was that he was so easy to get along with. Sometimes to a fault. If I wanted to eat Indian food, he went along. Stay home and call for Chinese? Fine. Campbell's tomato soup and sal-tines? A nod of his head. Sometimes I was tempted to just shake him:

"Tell me that you're in the mood for Ecuadorian food, if there is such a thing, or god-awful brown rice and steamed vegetables. Why do you always have to be so accommodating?" But what was the point? Create tension because there was none?

I reached up and tugged on a rebellious lock of his hair, then pushed back the little-boy bangs that flipped right down again. Chris was cute, everyone who met him thought so. He was also smart—smart enough in his quiet, sure way to dream up campaigns that brought clients millions of dollars. He was also modest. I remember how he told me, just in passing one day, that he had gotten perfect SAT scores. No wonder he had gotten into Yale and Princeton, even though he turned them down to go to Bard, a small, artsy school for brainy types who didn't fit the Ivy League mold.

We were a curious couple. I spent my days going through documents and public records, not to mention interviewing city and state officials to report on how an unending group of colorful characters tried to circumvent the law, all in the interest of telling readers the bald truth.

Chris, on the other hand, wrote the copy for print ads and TV commercials trying to seduce consumers by obscuring the truth or dismissing it entirely, to convince them what should and could be. Sometimes I was tempted to change places with him so that I could have fun dreaming up ways to get consumers into the stores to buy the newest condiment concoction or over-the-counter remedy for everything from PMS to acid reflux.

"Maybe we should change jobs," I said. "I'll come up with a campaign to sell black ketchup or Snapricot drink. You investigate the city parking violations bureau, and find out who's on the take."

"No thanks," Chris said. "Reality sucks."

"Reality sucks?" I guess I was in a dark mood because before I went shopping, I had to redo a column on deadline, which meant denying myself all food after eleven in the morning because I couldn't spare the time to go to the cafeteria, and barely made it to the bathroom to pee. Because I have this low-blood-sugar thing, I have to eat every couple of hours—or "graze" as they say—otherwise I turn short-tempered and hostile—well, even more than usual.

"The award-winning copywriter who brought us the Nike Nirvana campaign declares that he opts for fantasy, illusion and role playing rather than the world as it is? Thank you for negating my whole career and my whole life." Chris looked at me and narrowed his eyes slightly as if he was trying to figure out what I needed to hear.

"Do you want to eat a candy bar or take a nap or something, Jen?" he said, scratching the back of his neck.

"Candy is exactly what I don't want," I said, making my way toward the refrigerator for real food, even though we didn't have much because neither one of us had time to shop.

"And I don't need to take a nap," I said, like a cranky kid who did. "And don't change the subject."

"I'm not changing the subject," Chris said, holding up his hands helplessly and backing off. He went over to the refrigerator and took out a carton of Tropicana Grovestand orange juice, forgetting, as usual, to shake it, so that all the thick pulp remained at the bottom. He screwed off the orange plastic top and raised the container, about to start drinking directly from it.

"Oh my God, use a glass," I said. "That's so disgusting." I was starting to describe for the twentieth time how his germs would go back into the container to multiply, when he said, "Okay, okay," as he poured the last of it into a glass. He reached for another container and filled the glass to the top, then briefly played with the magnetic letters on the refrigerator door, rearranging them in a large arc pattern, spelling out the word C–R–I–S–I–S, the only word that ad agency types pay any attention to.

I was always amused to hear his colleagues ask, "Why is there never time to do it right, but always time to do it over?"

Chris took the glass of OJ, oblivious to the fact that he had poured it too full so the juice was swishing over the top as he sat in front of the TV. He put the glass down on the table, searching among our collection of remotes (the TV, the DVD, the VCR and the CD player), finally finding the right one, flipping it on and channel surfing until he landed at the six o'clock news. As usual, it was top heavy with sketchily reported stories of major traffic accidents, local fires and murders. We didn't quite finish the back-and-forth about reality versus fantasy, but there was no point in continuing, I had lost him.

That summed up the difference between men and women. He turned on the TV and I reached for the phone, sometimes more to hear my own voice than to talk to someone else. I had a colorful group of friends and depending on what was happening at the moment, I'd call the appropriate one. If all else failed, I called my mother.

Advice columnists sometimes tell you that it's healthy to argue. I suppose what they mean is that you keep the lines of communication open by voicing your differences rather than bottling them up. But Chris and I didn't argue. Whenever I brought up something controversial, he considered it momentarily and then seemed to decide that it wasn't worth raising his blood pressure over. In fact, he had very low-blood pressure, a medical marker of potentially long life. Chris was cool in every sense. That was usually fine with me, but sometimes, I guess, I just wanted him to take me by the hair and push his own agenda, so to speak. The only time that I could recall seeing him get really angry was when he went downstairs to the parking lot one day and saw that someone had dented the passenger door of his new grass-green Volkswagen bug, scraping off a strip of paint. He began yelling out a string of obscenities, like a ranting madman, until he was almost hoarse, kicking everything in sight until he ran out of steam, not to mention almost breaking his big toe. He had the car fixed, and never said another word about it, except that every time we went down to get the car, I know that he eyed it from every angle like a private detective about to dust for fingerprints.

Instead of picking on poor Chris anymore, I called Ellen Gaines, my former college roommate and best friend. First, I wanted to invite her to have dinner with us, and second, I needed to vent, something she understood particularly because she made a career of it. Ellen was a consumer reporter for ABC news and venting was her MO, in a nice way. It always amused me to watch her on TV where she looked not only perfectly coiffed, but also appeared to have this cool and controlled way of speaking, never raising her carefully modulated voice. Off the air, however, the reserve was put aside, and she could be as loud and abrasive as she wanted.

If someone had a grievance and had nowhere else to turn, they contacted Ellen's team, and if they were lucky enough to be one of the people that she and her staff had time to help, she inevitably got them satisfaction by holding the offenders up to public scrutiny. (It helps to shove a microphone in a scofflaw's face as he's on camera and ask him questions that he can't answer like, "How could you rent out an apartment with broken windows and rats running around it?" and taking prompt legal action if he failed to rectify things on his own.)

If only her own life was that simple. Ellen dated a succession of men, few of them leading to any long-term relationships. I was never sure whether she attracted dysfunctional guys or whether she was beaming out signals that said she didn't want to get involved. Then again maybe they simply assumed that as a consumer reporter, if they did anything wrong, especially to her, she'd have the might at her fingertips to cut them off at the knees—or worse.

The other possibility was that after spending day after day using the system to fight for the rights of the downtrodden, she had closed herself off to available men who came her way either by assuming that they had their private agendas or simply by feeling too mentally and physically exhausted from working twelve- or fourteen-hour days to even go out on a date and have a normal discussion.

I could understand that. There were days when my job totally sucked the lifeblood from me. No wonder some women on the ladder to success find themselves without husbands or even boyfriends, because a demanding career chips away at how much you have to give to someone else. There is just so much loving and nurturing in all of us, and sometimes our careers become our little children, demanding full-time attention, and requiring us to wipe noses and behinds.

Forget the image of superwoman; few of us can
do it all, or at least do it all very well. And the knowledge of that—especially if you are a perfectionist and
overachiever—always eats away at you and makes
you feel somehow compromised.

On Ellen's birthday, I couldn't resist buying her a
T-shirt from a Soho street vendor that said, Just Fuck
Off.

"Whose rear did you save today?" I said when
Ellen answered.

"Not my own. Never complain again when your
shower isn't hot enough or when your super takes
too long to turn on the air-conditioning. We sent a
crew up to a rat-infested tenement in Harlem where
the windows have holes in them big enough for a
cat to crawl through and the water in the pipes is so
rusty you can't wash dishes."

Maybe Chris was right, reality did suck. "So what
did you do?"

"Well now, after six months, we're forcing the
landlord to do repairs and in the meantime we're
moving the family into a hotel."

"You did good," I said, immediately forgetting
about my gripes and feeling small for needing to vent
about what was eating me.

"Yes, for one family," Ellen said, "after months of
calls and intervention by the city. But what about the
others who live in those burnt-out joints and never
bother to contact consumer reporters for help be-

cause they've given up on everybody and everything or simply don't know how to navigate the system?"

"You save the world one person at a time," I said, reaching for an old cliché. "If you dwell on the extent of the job, you'll be paralyzed. But to change the subject, you sound like you could use a break, so how about joining me and Chris for dinner? His old roommate is in town."

"Now you're trying to save me," she said, exhaling. "A *blind* date?"

"He's not blind," I said. "And you have to eat anyway."

There was silence on the other end of the line.

"Well?"

"Fine," Ellen said. "But let's not talk about what *I* do, okay? Last time we double-dated I woke up the next morning and found that he had slipped his résumé under my door along with several letters of recommendation."

I didn't remember that. "Why?"

"He wanted to get out of law and break into TV journalism. He thought, it was 'sexier.' And if they don't want to change careers, they start telling me about how their banks screwed them, how the dry cleaner burned their suit, or how they couldn't cash a traveler's check without two forms of ID, even though it's the same thing as cash." She had my sympathy there. Everyone who had a particular beef usually ended up sharing it with a friend from the media.

"Then there was the guy who thought that when you were fixing him up with an action reporter you meant a journalist who put out," Ellen said. I never doubted that if she left TV she could become a stand-up comic.

We arranged to meet for dinner on Saturday. What I didn't tell her was that Chris's former roommate, who I hadn't met because he lived in upstate New York, wasn't like the other guys that she knew.

"What's his name?" she asked, almost as an after-thought.

I paused for a minute. "His name…"

"His name, yes… Is that such a hard question?"

"Moose," I mumbled.

Silence. "*What?* What did you say?"

"Moose."

"Is he one?" Ellen said, cracking up.

"No…he's not an animal. He just lives up in the Adirondacks to be near them. Likes wildlife more than city people."

"Oh," Ellen said, considering that. "I can understand *that.*"

I started to hang up, when I heard her call my name.

"Jenny?"

"What?" I said, lifting the receiver back up to my ear.

"You're not fixing me up with some freaky loner like Ted Kaczynski, are you?"

"The Unabomber?"

"Yeah."

"Oh please," I said. "Definitely not. He lived in Montana. Moose lives in upstate New York."

"Oh," Ellen said. "That sets my mind at ease."

Chapter Three

On a regular basis I get one or two angry letters from readers complaining that the media always dwells on what is "base and unsavory about the human condition, and that it can never find good news to report," as one reader put it. I thought about that and with Christmas approaching and a warm, generous spirit warming my soul as the holiday got closer, I put off a column about major fraud in a prestigious Manhattan co-op in favor of a column about what was working well in New York and what reflected its essential goodness. I wrote up a charitable group that came to the aid of homebound people in need; animal shelters that had gone from kill to no-kill, and a group of college graduates who banded together to renovate houses for the poor on the Lower East Side. That brought a few favorable calls, and a pound of homemade dog-shaped short-bread cookies (for human consumption, I assumed) from an animal rights group.

Slaid was obviously feeling less charitable. His column zeroed in on accounting discrepancies between what a major charity reported and what it actually took in and the fact that the authorities had found that the chairman had a criminal record. He described the widening investigation hinting at indictments to come. A coup for him, but I was above calling him to take potshots at his reporting, particularly his obvious failure to respect a news embargo. But I'd be big about that, let it slide. I considered sending him the cookies, but decided against it, once I tasted them.

Of course, I could have taken the opportunity to call and demonstrate my largesse—simply congratulate him. Christmas was in the air, why be mean-spirited? It was a nice piece of reporting and we were all working for the common good. But he'd never accept my praise at face value. He would ponder my real agenda, so I held back.

So what did the high-brow columnist do? He called up and started making barking noises—combining the bark of a Lab with the howl of a beagle. Can I swear that it was him? No, but I racked my brains to think of who else might have stooped to that level and I came up dry. Rather than dignify the call with a reaction of any sort, I hung up, annoyed, and left my desk to escape to Bloomingdale's, this time to buy myself a gift or two.

Bloomingdale's is a place where you can lose yourself for hours. And even if you have one of those days when every garment you pick makes a mockery of your face and body, you can always find a pair of Pumas in a scrumptious new space age–type design or color combination; treat yourself to a jar of something heavenly like Origins White Tea body cream, or at the very least, find solace in a quick cup of vegetable soup and half a tuna sandwich or a large dish of custardlike yogurt with health pretensions downstairs at the in-store restaurant called Forty Carrots.

I started my outing by going through the aisles of costume jewelry, trying on various Tahitian pearl-wanna-be necklaces, and wondering what it would feel like to wear the real thing. Then, even though I rarely wear earrings, I tried on dangly chandelier styles, hoping that they would help liberate that uninhibited part of me that lurked close to the surface. After that charade was over, I headed upstairs like a kid in a candy store to lingerie, my weakness. I examined bras, thongs and string bikinis as delicate as snowflakes, looking for my favorite brands, Natori, Hanro and Cose Belle. Now I'm in my element. It amazes me how just a few ounces of the right underwear can make one's sexuality confidence soar. I'm hoping that a few new purchases will make

Chris's head swivel from the TV to me as I undress in front of him in lingerie that if calculated by the pound, probably costs about three hundred and fifty dollars.

Never for a moment do I forget that he could as easily have chosen to live with someone who was a decade younger, not to mention firmer. A career that has you sitting for ten hours a day has cumulative effects. It's not that I'm what you would call fat. I'm not. It's just that everything could benefit from a large body stocking that would cinch it all in, raise it up just a tad, and overall smooth out the flesh.

So half an hour later, I've collected four thongs— fuchsia, petal pink, black and navy, and matching demi bras with just the slightest layer of padding that do an amazing job of creating impressive cleavage so that the unsuspecting would immediately assume that I'm a 36C rather than a 34B.

Then I'm on to nightgowns. I spy a plain, ivory-colored silk slip-style nightgown and hold it up in front of me in the mirror, trying to decide whether it's classically simple and elegant, or simply dull and sexless. I stare into the mirror, but it's a tough call, not to mention that the fluorescent light is turning my skin a coordinating shade of jaundiced yellow.

As I'm studying myself in the mirror with the gown pressed up against me, in my peripheral vision I pick up the outline of a man in a black leather jacket. I have to confess that one of my pet peeves is seeing men lingering about awkwardly in the women's lingerie department. It's not that they're not entitled to be there. Or that they don't actually belong there. They might be buying gifts for women or accompanying girlfriends on shopping outings or what have you, and legally their presence is as defensible as mine is. Still, this little catty voice in the back of my head keeps saying, "Oh, get out of here, you're invading my privacy." I do get some consolation, however, from the fact that at least some of the men look away when you stare at them because they're uncomfortable and feel out of place.

So those kinds of thoughts were swirling around in my head as I gazed at myself. I tried to ignore the image and turned back to the nightgown, holding it this way and that, but then the image moved closer, and then closer, until he was almost next to me and I was about to pivot and yell out for security.

At the sound of a low wolf whistle, I looked back, startled. He was leaning up against the corner of the mirrored column, black eyeglasses now pushed up on the top of his head.

"Yes?" I said in a too-loud voice, intended to alert fellow shoppers to beware as well.

"Jenny George," said a low teasing voice.

It took me several seconds to realize I was staring at the face I had seen only in the newspaper that appeared with his column.

"Slaid Warren," I cooed back, moving only my eyes, leaving the nightgown pressed against me.

He tilted his head to the side, as if in judgment, holding my gaze. "Your picture doesn't do you justice."

I smiled briefly, to trivialize the compliment, not knowing how else to handle it. He was right about the picture. I photographed like a deer caught in the headlights.

"Is this where you usually hang out after work?" I said, trying to gloss over my discomfort. He leaned over to whisper in my ear.

"If I can't actually slip behind the velvet curtains."

I turned back to him and studied him briefly— noting the worn jeans teamed with a black cashmere sweater and black leather Pumas. But while I was surveying his outfit, the silky nightgown slipped from my grasp. We nearly collided as we simultaneously kneeled down to get it. He got there first, and handed it to me, amused by my discomfort.

"Thanks," I said, pulling it back to me. "Nice to see you," I said, unable to come up with anything better than a platitude. I turned abruptly toward the cashier ready to pay for the nightgown, although at that point I had decided the thing was plain, boring and matronly and that I didn't want it. I considered telling him to keep away from dressing rooms or he'd be the subject of my next column, but then decided to keep quiet and head off without starting up a dialogue.

"Wait," he said, reaching out to touch my arm to stop me. "I want to show you something." He led me over to a designer rack and took out a long, low-cut charcoal-gray silk nightgown with a deeply cut back that was held together with delicate crisscross laces of pale yellow satin. He held it up to me.

"This is the one that will knock your guy's socks off," he said with a small smile on his face. To be honest, it was heavenly, beautiful and sexy in an elegant, sophisticated way that nearly made me swoon. If I had seen it I would have grabbed it.

"Hmm," I said. "Not bad." He nodded. I looked at the price tag, then shook my head. "Can't afford it. They must pay more generously at the *Trib.*"

"A gift from me," he said, starting to lead me to the cashier with his platinum card in hand. "A peace offering."

"No thanks," I said. "I wouldn't want anyone to think that I was sleeping with the competition."

"I wouldn't either. I'm all for the naked truth."

I looked back at him briefly and then looked away, swiping the nightgown from his hand and hanging it back on the rack. He picked it up again and tossed it over his shoulder.

"Too nice to pass up," he said. "I'll buy it for a friend."

"Lucky girl," I said, regretting the words just a nanosecond after I said them, knowing how he'd misinterpret them.

He nodded, amused.

"Well, merry Christmas," I said, scooping up the underwear that I had tried to hide beneath my handbag. I was about to head across the floor to another register to pay.

He pointedly stared at the underwear that was squished up in my fist and narrowed his eyes.

"Lucky guy," he whispered, then walked off the other way.

Chapter Four

"So where do we have dinner with a mountain man who probably eats grilled roadkill for dinner?" I asked Chris when I got home from Bloomingdale's.

"Moose?"

"Who else?"

"He's easy," Chris said. "He eats meat when he has to, but he prefers vegetarian."

"Hmm," I said. I thought of a local health-food restaurant, but then remembered the soy burger that I had there that tasted as if it was made from corrugated paper. Mexican? We could have fajitas with beans and rice and guacamole—and margaritas.

"He does drink," I said, more as a statement than a question.

"Everything except the worm in the mescal," Chris said. We agreed to meet at a Mexican restaurant in the Village. Characteristically, Chris and I walked. Since both of us spent our days sitting and didn't have much time to exercise, we looked forward to a chance to take long walks together. Even when we weren't talking, we usually felt very much in sync. I knew when he was quiet, he was absorbing things around him, which usually ended up, in one form or another, in one of his ads or TV commercials. There were talking beagles in a commercial for dog food that reminded me of the sad brother and sister up for adoption in the neighborhood pet store. In a commercial for packaged deli meat, Chris incorporated a character with black beady eyes and curly hair who looked like a man who worked in Todaro, our favorite Italian grocery.

"Life is all ad copy," he said. I knew what he meant. Half of the things I experienced day to day worked into upcoming columns. We walked down First Avenue past Bellevue Hospital and New York University Hospital and then past apartment complexes. Chris thought of what he could use in commercials for pain relievers, while for me, the scenery triggered thoughts of the latest hospital mergers, Medicaid and the best emergency room to go for gunshot wounds.

"When was the last time you saw Moose?"

"I visited him a couple of years ago," Chris said. "He had just split with his girlfriend and was having a tough time, so we went skiing during the day and drank a lot of beer at night."

"It must be hard for him to meet the kind of women who'd like the same lifestyle that he does."

"Just the opposite," Chris said. "Women love his mountain life—at least for a while. They're fed up with the big-city bullshit. Land is cheap, you have all the space and quiet that you want, and you only concern yourself with the basics, like survival. You don't go to four-star restaurants, you don't go out to Broadway shows. You don't run down the street and shop at Victoria's Secret." (How did he know?) "You're together a lot at home working on your house or cooking and canning and doing blue-collar stuff, so you find out very fast if you're compatible."

"So what happened to his relationship?"

"I guess when the initial fascination faded, she felt cut off and she wasn't pulling her weight."

The image of a woman as a member of a dogsled team came to mind. "What do you mean?"

"He wanted to share his life and for Moose that means someone who could help him cut down trees for firewood and build an addition to the house. She liked to cook and help him fix up the house, but that was it."

"You mean she couldn't even chop down trees?"

He nodded, laughing.

"He's liberated—to a fault," I said.

Chris shrugged. "He has a lot to give, but he hasn't found a girl who's big enough to take it." I thought about Ellen. I hoped that wouldn't be a big mistake, unless he wanted someone to stand by him to fight with local industry about polluting the air or water.

When we got to the restaurant, neither one of them was there yet so we sat down in a booth and ordered a pitcher of frozen pomegranate margaritas. After sipping half of one, I started to forget about Moose and Ellen.

"We should do this more at home," I said to Chris. His knees touched mine under the table and he reached down and took my hand.

"You're wasted already?"

I started to laugh. I spotted Ellen as she walked in, but then wasn't sure if I was waving at the right girl. Something was different, and then I realized that I was seeing more of her face. The haircut was short and almost boyish, an impossible style for most women, but on Ellen it looked delicate, pixieish and feminine, not to mention that the red color looked richer than I remembered. It framed her face and pale complexion. Ellen is five-four with big blue expressive eyes. She's almost thirty-three, but could pass for ten years younger. I think it's because she works mostly indoors, away from the sun. With less hair, her eyes seemed to pop.

"Love the hair," I said as she took a seat. She smiled.

"I cut it off because I was fed up, but it turns out that everybody likes it. At work they call me Peter Pan."

Chris poured her a drink and she sat back and sipped it and then shook her head. "I had a day...I'm beginning to doubt—except for present company—that there are any honest, upstanding citizens in the world."

"There aren't," I said flatly. "That's why we'll never run out of copy." Ellen just shook her head.

"What are you working on?" Chris asked her.

"Shabby contractors, bogus long-distance phone charges, car complaints, spoiled dog food, unsafe toys..." She shook her head. "I could go on and on."

I looked up to see a giant standing next to our table wearing a thick suede jacket. He was bearlike, maybe six foot five, with a beard and brown curly hair.

"Hey," Chris said, coming around the table and hugging him the way men do, in a hard, standoffish kind of way. It reminded me of a Broadway play that I saw years back called *Defending the Caveman* that homed in on the differences between the sexes, showing in one particular scene how old female friends greet each other, as opposed to the male approach. Women squeal in delighted high-pitched voices and then come together screeching, laughing, crying and embracing. And men? One goes up to the other and punches him in the arm while saying something endearing like: "You still driving that old piece of shit?"

Moose patted him on the back. "How you doing?" Chris introduced him to me and then to Ellen.

"Ladies," he said, nodding.

Chris poured him a drink and we toasted. I looked at Chris, then at Moose. His blue eyes peered out, surrounded by curly locks as though he were Santa. The immediate impression that I got was of shyness.

"How come you're in town?" I said.

"Came to see my mom. I can't get her to come up and visit me…" He shrugged and didn't finish the sentence.

"It's pretty cold up there," I said, feeling for some reason as if I had to take her side.

"Twenty below last week," he said matter-of-factly.

"So you live in an igloo?" Ellen teased.

Moose shook his head as if he had considered that and then decided against it. "Log cabin. I built it. Great woodstove, keeps the place really warm."

"What do you do all winter?" I said. "Doesn't it get lonely?"

He looked at me curiously and smiled slightly. "I have work to do in the house, firewood to cut, I'm preparing to put on an addition, and I have my books, carpentry work in town, journals, my dog and I'm writing a guide to wilderness survival. Not much time to get lonely."

"Wilderness survival?" Ellen said.

Actually, it turned out that he was working on his third book. Ever since he was small, Moose said, he spent most of his life outdoors. After we looked at our menus and ordered he told us that his mother was a nature lover who grew up on a farm and unlike other mothers who baked, cleaned, shopped and maybe went off to work, she spent much of her time with her children outdoors, hiking, swimming in the ponds, and teaching them about birds, snakes, turtles, insects, trees and plants. By age ten, he was an expert marksman with a slingshot and a bow and arrow, he knew how to start a fire, build a shelter and forage for food, distinguishing between the edible plants and berries and the poisonous ones so that he could basically survive outdoors, no matter what the temperature. He learned how to carve plates out of wood polished with beaver fat and could weave baskets out of split white oak, make his own clothes and get by in the woods with just some basic clothes and a knife.

That was a world that, of course, was unknown to me. I never did understand all the esoterica about camping and being able to use a compass if I was lost, build a tent for shelter or cook over an open fire.

That's not to say I wouldn't welcome being in the wilderness with the right guide, particularly if he looked like the six-foot-four Australian who took me and a group of friends on a rafting trip in Colorado, our present to ourselves after we graduated from college.

"So you spent your summers camping out?" Ellen asked Moose.

"I camped outside my house from the age of eight," Moose said. "My parents built me a tepee in the backyard instead of a tree house and I spent most of the year out there. I grew my own fruits and vegetables in the garden and made my own clothes. Even my own shoes."

Ellen and I looked at each other. Manolo of the Adirondacks.

"And I bet you never went to the doctor," I said.

"To get my shots and all, sure. But when I was sick I tried to treat myself with medicine from plants. I haven't been to the doctor in the past twenty years."

"Germs probably can't survive where you live," I said. He smiled.

"And what about when you're doing all that outdoor work. Don't you ever fall or hurt yourself?" Ellen asked.

"I broke my ankle a few years ago. Set it myself."

We were all silent. I was proud of myself when I closed a wound with ointment and a butterfly bandage.

"So you're writing your book with a quill pen, or what?" I said. He shook his head.

"I have a computer and all that. I'm connected." I imagined him hunkering down by candlelight and writing on a computer.

"Let me guess," I said. "You built your own with twigs and leaves."

"Actually I have a Dell," Moose said, laughing. "But now that you mention it…" With a smile he steered the subject to me, obviously eager to get himself out of the spotlight. "So what about you, how are you doing with the column?"

"The pressure gets me a little crazy," I said. "But I couldn't imagine doing anything else."

"I read your stuff from time to time online," he said. "I try to keep up with the papers."

"We don't cover your part of the world that much. Any good investigations to be done where you are?"

He was silent for a moment. "Local political stuff, sure, but it's a small town and people tend to get along."

"And if they don't?"

"They don't go running to the media."

"Sounds idyllic," Ellen said.

"What do you do?" Moose asked Ellen. She reached into her bag and gave him her card. Moose looked at it and smiled slightly.

"Consumer reporter," he read. "That raises your blood pressure."

"I try not to let it," Ellen said. He stared at her for a long minute and didn't say anything.

"How long you been doing it?"

"Six years," she said. She looked back at me. "Remember when I took the job?"

I couldn't forget. It was a year after she started with the network. She was nervous and we arranged to have lunch at 21 to celebrate, even though most of the time she talked about all the reasons why she secretly felt she wasn't up to the job, couldn't do it and shouldn't have agreed to take it. With all the negativity out of the way, we agreed never to have another conversation like that, ate every bit of the amazing hamburgers that the place is famous for— each seemed to be made up of at least half a pound of meat—finished off most of a bottle of very expensive wine and had to practically hold hands to steady ourselves as we walked across Fifth Avenue and over to Saks to buy her clothes that would look good on television.

"We didn't think you'd stay there for more than two years," I said. "Six is a record."

Ellen nodded resignedly.

"So what keeps you going when everyone else burns out?" Chris asked.

"Venom," Ellen said, "and determination. I can't let the bastards win."

Moose nodded, weighing that. "But there are more of them," he added. "So at some point you have to stop and concentrate on fixing your own head."

"Is your head fixed?" she asked, confronting Moose. "Are you balanced? Normal?"

"I've never been accused of being normal," he laughed. "But I'm better than I was," he said, continuing to look at Ellen. The waiter brought the food and we all stopped talking as he set it in front of us.

"Guess you don't eat like this too much in the mountains," Chris said to Moose.

He shook his head. "I used to live with a girl who liked to cook," he said, then shrugged. "Since then, I make do." He looked down at himself and laughed. "Doesn't look like I'm starving, does it?" Ellen smiled at Moose, a real smile. I poked Chris with my foot, under the table. He glanced at me questioningly for a second.

"Listen, I don't know what your timing is," he said to Moose. "But I'm probably getting some concert tickets next weekend for a group that's getting big around here." He looked at Ellen and then back at Moose. "If you guys want to join us, I can get two more tickets."

Every once in a while Chris surprises me with how fast he can operate. I suppose that was why at work he was able to focus at a crucial moment and create something that was right on target for his audience.

"Sure," Moose said. "I'm going to be here through the week."

"Anything that gets my mind off what I do," Ellen said, unusually upbeat.

"Great," Chris said. "Saturday then." We ordered flan and Mexican cheesecake and then talked about

Adirondack life, hiking in the snow, cooking dinner on an open fire under the stars, and then sleeping in a tent with down sleeping bags made to withstand temperatures up to 20 degrees below. Moose didn't camp out in winter, but even in the summer, temperatures at night and in the early morning can get down into the 50s, sometimes dropping dramatically as the wind picked up.

By the end of dinner, I think all of us were ready to drive home with him to explore an alternative way of living. We walked outside and Chris and I headed to First Avenue to go home.

"I'm going up Lexington," Ellen said to Moose.

"So am I," he said. "Do you want company?" They turned and walked off together and I watched them from a distance. Moose was a foot taller, if you counted the mop of curly hair.

"He's a sweet guy," I said to Chris.

"Sweet?" he hesitated. "Hmm…on one level. But on another…" He paused again. "He's the most determined, tough-minded, independent son of a bitch." I listened to Chris and didn't say anything. It was one thing to hear it from a guy, and another to get a female perspective.

When we got home, we undressed and fell into bed and made love in a soft, easy way—part comfortable affection, part margaritas making my blood cells feel as though they were dancing. I was about to fall asleep, when I thought of Ellen. She was close to my age, but still, I felt as though she was my little sister. Did Moose walk her all the way home? Did she ask him in for a drink? She spent her life fighting to help other people get by. Why did I think that I had to watch out for her?

"What were the other women in Moose's life like?" I asked Chris.

"I can only remember one," he said sleepily. I waited, but he didn't say anything.

"I think you told me about her, but I've forgotten what you said."

Chris rolled over and I could tell from the sound of his breathing that he was about to fall asleep. It never took him more than twenty seconds. He could fall asleep standing on the subway. I was insanely jealous. I needed total darkness, quiet, even the right temperature. And if there was a faucet dripping...

"CHRIS..."

"What?" he said, jumping up as though I had startled him.

"What was she like?"

"Who?"

"The girl he was seeing," I said.

"Hot," he said.

"So what happened?"

"Do we have to talk about this now," he mumbled.

Why, at one in the morning, when I should have been concerned about falling asleep, was I wondering about the love life of a mountain man? Ellen hadn't even dated him, and for all I knew, she wasn't even interested.

I don't know about you, but I feel as though for my entire life I've been wasting my own time, not to mention that of friends and family trying to figure out why men act the way they do. And what they're looking for.

Chapter Five

"Who was she?" I asked Chris a few minutes later.

"An actress," he said. "Pretty famous, I think, but he never told me." Trivia expert that I am, my brain scanned all the names of the current actresses who might have traveled up to the Adirondacks to do a film or prepare for one, and then, thanks to my devotion to gossip columns and celebrity trivia, bingo, it hit me.

I never saw the movie. It was some type of out-ward-bound-thriller flick where something goes terribly wrong. I don't remember whether the girl gets chased by a bear, or whether her food supplies are invaded by a mountain lion and her campsite ransacked or whatever, but fear gets the better of her and she has a breakdown. Because of it, she packs up and goes home to her cushy New England life a changed woman from the spoiled princess who left. The actress that they cast in the role was a young, blue-eyed ingenue who, I read, spent three months in the area learning survival skills to prepare for the role.

Clearly, I was jumping the gun, but it was one of those intuitive moments when you just know something, so I was willing to swear that Kelly Cartwright was the girl who had been Moose's live-in. After I was sure that Chris was deep asleep, I crept out of bed and sat down at my computer.

I went from one site to another and finally found some bios of her and magazine articles that described how she prepared for the role.

The article discussed how she read every book she could find on wilderness survival and made an extended trip up to the Adirondacks to talk to hiking guides, campers, outdoorsmen and survivalists to learn about getting along outdoors, alone, in the company of four-legged friends such as bears, moose, mountain lions and God knows what else.

So, enter Moose. Even though I never saw his name mentioned in any of the articles, how could K.C. not be the one that he was seeing? I mean, how many guys like him were there who got involved with a movie star?

Two in the morning. Should I call Ellen? No, dumb idea. What if Moose was there with her? And if he wasn't, she'd be in a dead sleep. I bookmarked the sites, and then slid back into bed. Chris rolled over toward me and slipped his arm around me. I snuggled up next to him and fell asleep.

"Kelly Cartwright? Is she the one who looks like an eighteen-year-old Robin Wright Penn?" Ellen asked. When I finally reached her on Monday. Why was it that every celebrity was described as looking like somebody else, as if there was a limited gene pool from which all players were created? It was similar to the way book reviewers described authors. They were always crosses between two or three others—Hemingwayesque, or Shavian, Faulknerian—who wrote in the same genre, as if no one was original and every work was merely a crazy quilt of what had come before.

"Well, a younger Robin Wright Penn," I said, "but not as good an actress."

"Mmm, I thought she was miscast in *Hometown Queen,*" Ellen said. It was clear why we were friends. "She didn't have the breadth of character to carry it off."

"Agreed," I said. Still, we were getting ahead of ourselves. Two plus two didn't equal ten.

"Any number of people could have helped her for the role, and it was quite possible that she wasn't the one at all," Ellen said. "Maybe some celebrity just went up there looking for property. You know how they always want to buy houses in places like upstate New York, Montana, Wyoming or up-and-coming spots like Marfa, Texas, where no one would run into them."

But the more I thought about it, the more convinced I became.

"I know it's her," I said, and then changed the subject back to Moose. "So what happened with him?"

"He came back here and we sat on the floor talking about everything from television to books to seasons for planting," Ellen said. "He even went outside to examine the garden in the back of the building and we talked about starting a vegetable garden," she said. "Then we went through a bottle of wine."

"And?"

"He left at two," Ellen said. I couldn't tell whether she was relieved or disappointed.

"Did he want to?"

"Well, he didn't jump me, if that's what you mean."

He already got four stars for good behavior. "Did he act interested?"

"Well…we talked for two hours," she said. "But the crazy thing is, I think he was trying to pretend that he wasn't interested."

"Well, that'll make it better when it does happen," I said.

"Maybe," Ellen said. "I don't know."

"Did he say he'd call before we go to the concert?"

"No. He just smiled and said he'd better push off." She paused. "But he has my card…."

★ ★ ★

When Chris walked in from work, I told him about Moose and Ellen.

"If he jumped her bones she would have resented it," he said, peeling off his jacket and tossing it on the couch. "So he played it cool and that put her off? We can't win."

"Well, I just thought he might have said something—'I'll call you,' or whatever—to let her know that he was interested," I said, jumping to Ellen's defense. "I think he's the first guy that she's had an iota of interest in in the last six months. I know she probably wouldn't admit it, but I could tell. I saw a sparkle in her eye that I haven't seen since you know who."

"So let her make a move on him," he said, sinking onto the couch. "She's a big girl."

"Do you like it when a woman comes on to you?"

Major shoulder shrug. "Depends who," he said. "Yeah, why not?"

I dropped down on top of him and tried to pin his arms above his head. "This okay?" I said.

He laughed. "Yeah, definitely."

Men always said they wanted women to come on to them, but that didn't make it true. While initially it flattered the hell out of them if a woman pursued them, after the first date, most men liked to take charge. If the relationship wasn't on their terms, it made them uneasy.

"How's the diet-drink campaign going?" I said, dropping the subject.

He shrugged. "We've been brainstorming, but I don't have anything yet.

"What's your deadline?"

He massaged his temples. "Forty-eight hours." He picked up the TV page of the paper, scanned it, and then grabbed the remote and started to channel surf. When I first met Chris it surprised me to see him come home from work and spend most of the night in front of the TV when he had a deadline the next morning. I thought he'd be sitting in front of the computer, or staring at pictures of the product. Only later did I realize that he really wasn't watching television as much as using it to help him think. It became the backdrop for the movie that he was making in his head. Maybe he needed the visual wallpaper to stimulate his thinking.

I was the opposite. The blare of radio or TV destroyed my concentration, which may explain why we had the different kinds of jobs that we did. Clearly, he was a right-brain kind of guy—holistic, random and intuitive, and I was a left-brain—more logical, analytical and sequential.

I slipped out of the room and went into the kitchen to start making dinner, something that I didn't do on a regular basis. It wasn't that I didn't like to cook, it was just that I didn't want to fall into a routine that would regularly take a chunk out of my day and that wasn't, as I saw it, effective in terms of the time spent cooking/time spent eating it ratio.

But tonight at least, I wanted to help Chris in any way that I could. I really sympathized with him. The pressure of having to produce under a deadline could make the most secure person crumble. I took out a steak, made a marinade, and then let it sit for a while before putting it under the broiler. I put baked potatoes into the microwave and cut up a salad. When the steak was ready—rare for him, medium-well for me—I brought a tray over to the coffee table. He turned to me for a minute, intuiting the moral support that I hoped to be offering along with the food.

"Thanks," he said, turning back to the TV. He cut into the meat and ate like a hungry dog. I sat next to him, amused, and we watched a mindless quiz show followed by an episode of *Animal Planet*. Were we melding into a Middle American couple? But no, there was no *TV Guide* on the coffee table, no popcorn or even Bud Light. And I'm proud to say that there were no Barcaloungers in our living room and never would be, despite the fact that the horrendous-looking things were amazingly comfortable. But there we were, not exchanging as much as a word for the entire time we sat in front of the TV. Finally, Chris turned to me.

"Metamorphosis?

"You're kidding, right?"

"Yeah," he said, giving me his signature half smile. We sat there for another minute without speaking.

"How about 'The Change'?" I said.

"You're kidding, right?"

"Yeah." We sat some more. How ridiculous was this? Two mature adults trying to come up with the name of a diet drink that would be no more effective than a low-fat malted but at twice the price. Who could give up food for any length of time without going back to it with a vengeance that would ultimately negate all the weight lost while enduring sweet diet drinks instead of real meals. I thought of "Fraud," but thought better of suggesting it. Maybe "Waste." Those who couldn't spell might think that it would give them one.

"Slice of Life," I said brightly, starting to toss out ideas and brainstorming. "Close Shave. Beanpole, Svelte, Stick, Stick Figure, Slim, Shape—oops, forget that, they already used that—ummm…" More silence. But then, in a flash of inspiration, I knew that I had it.

"Wait," I said suddenly. "I've got your name."

He looked at me. "Well?"

I nodded my head up and down. "I have it, it's great, really great." He held out his hands.

"So?"

I thought I'd torture him for a bit. I was a superhero to the rescue. The pressure was off, Chris was home free and tomorrow he'd be a star in the client's eyes thanks to yours truly.

"Yep, it's really great. Really, really fresh, original. This one will bring you a raise. Maybe even a Clio."

"So what the hell is it?" he asked, losing patience.

The pregnant pause. "Model Thin," I said softly with a self-satisfied expression on my face. And again for more emphasis. "Model Thin."

"Hmm," Chris said in a positive voice, nodding his head slightly. I had struck a nerve. "Hmm," he said again, biting the corner of his thumbnail. "That's not bad. That is definitely not bad at all."

"Think of all the models that you could hire for the shoot," I said, regretting the words the instant they rolled off my tongue. He sat there, mulling it over.

"I could work with that," Chris said. "Model Thin."

"Can we go out and take a walk now?" I said. "I'm getting tired of vegging out in front of the TV." He clicked it off decisively and we headed out, walking downtown, toward the Village, always a good destination because it was about three miles there and back. We stopped at a coffee bar for espresso and pastries that would never allow me to become model thin, scanned magazines and out-of-town newspapers hanging along a wooden rack on the wall, and then got up to leave. As we got outside, fate reared its head, and a six-foot-tall blonde strutted by. Perfect skin,

What Men Want

hair piled sloppily on top of her head, arresting blue eyes and, of course, she was totally without makeup, which I can't stand because it tells me that that's how she looks in the morning or the middle of the night if, say, she runs out to the street because her house is on fire.

I looked her up and down. Never mind the ragged jeans that are made to look grungy, so unappealing to me, and the tired-looking down jacket, she was ready for the cover of *Vogue*. If she wasn't a model yet, she'd be discovered in a heartbeat. She just had that camera-ready look—you can always tell.

"Model Thin," Chris said, looking right into her eyes. "I like that." She looked at him curiously and then just smiled. I took his hand and pulled him away, in the direction of uptown, trying to ignore the knot eating into the base of my stomach.

Chapter Six

There is no shortage of stories for my column, only a shortage of waking hours to write about them and all the colorful characters who enjoy operating outside the law. Someone on the rewrite desk here once said that after people who are in public office finish serving their terms, they should go directly to jail for the same amount of time that they were in office. My sentiments exactly. In fact, on my wall I had a blow up of the "Go to Jail" square from the Monopoly board. Around it I arranged pictures of various felons who I had written about.

I was coming up in the elevator one morning when I overheard a conversation that made my ears perk up. An editor from the travel section was chatting with a colleague. He had just come back from St. Croix, he said, where he'd checked out some new resorts. He mentioned that he had seen someone that he knew from the Mayor's Office of Film, Theatre and Broadcasting. The editor asked him if he was on vacation and he said no, he was there on business. They laughed about it, but I didn't see the humor. Instead, my antennae went up. Business? Who was he meeting? And why in St. Croix? Call it my reporter's instinct for a big story but I went back to my desk and started making phone calls.

I'd heard rumors some time back about Caribbean trips, but at the time I had been so swamped that I didn't pay any attention to them. But now, if it came up again, it convinced me that it was something that I should look into. Were people in the mayor's office on film purportedly meeting Hollywood producers to encourage them to bring big-budget films to the city? More and more these days, American films were being made in Canada because of the considerable financial savings due to the favorable exchange rate. But while the goals of people in the film office might have been honorable, there was no justification for spending taxpayers' money for meetings in the Caribbean that could well have taken place in New York. Clearly, New York wanted and benefited from having movie studios use the city as home base for their filming. New York City's Made In New York Incentive Program offered film and TV crews tax and marketing credits as well as customer services if most of the movies were made in the five boroughs. But there was a line between proper give-and-take and giving out bigger pieces of the tax-deduction pie to some studios and not others. City negotiators were not supposed to be for sale to the highest bidder.

And why have a meeting at a resort in St. Croix instead of a Lower Manhattan conference room, other than to acquire a tan? Couldn't the information be gathered in writing or via conference calls? Was it really critical to go to the Caribbean? A colder view of it was that the city officials were taking their wives or girlfriends with them on free junkets that would turn into improper deals.

My phone book was filled with the names of disgruntled employees from almost every city agency, and I made my initial string of phone calls rounding up "the usual suspects"—people you can usually count on to talk in sound bites and give you dependable quotes and insights.

I heard snickers, guffaws, theatrical coughs. Did they know more than they let on? I imagined eyebrows being raised, but none of that could make an airtight story. Trying a different tack, I called officials from the previous administration and asked them about conferences outside of the city.

"Does Brooklyn count?" one aide responded. "Because that's as far as I ever traveled on the city payroll." Someone else pointed me to an airline employee who would check the passenger lists to see whether the mayor's aides had flown regularly scheduled airlines—or instead hopped free flights on corporate jets belonging to Hollywood movie studios, which might be offered sweet deals to bring their crews into the city for months at a time.

I spent the morning making phone calls, and then bingo, just before I was about to leave, I got a call back from an employee of a boutique hotel in the Caribbean who confirmed that several city employees were already staying there, supposedly to attend a film production conference.

"I don't have any conference rooms booked," he said. "But there's a big buffet dinner and beach party tonight. Maybe meetings are going on in private suites. That often happens."

"Beach party," I repeated, as a statement, not a question. The words stuck in my craw.

"Yes," he said. "We have outdoor grills and set up tables facing the water—"

"I know," I said tolerantly. I thought of how much was deducted for city and state taxes on my last paycheck and I saw red. I grabbed my notebook and knocked on the glass partition of my editor's door. He waved me in.

"Marty," I said. He turned his florid face up to me. He was wearing his usual blue oxford button-down shirt with the sleeves rolled up and a blue print tie that was perpetually loose and askew. There was always a half-finished paper cup filled with coffee on his desk. He motioned to a chair facing his desk and I fell back into it.

"It looks as though some of the mayor's people are down in the Caribbean supposedly on business. This has come up before, and I think it's a pattern." I had his attention. He pushed his chair back from his desk and folded his arms across his chest.

"How do you know?"

"It started with a conversation in the elevator. John Carey from travel was down in St. Croix. Then I made some calls and found out that three or four of the people from the mayor's film office are down there."

"Any idea who they're meeting with?"

"All I could find out is that there's a corporate jet from a leading production house called Reilly Films parked at the airport."

"Call travel and go down there," he said, turning back to his screen. That surprised me. It usually took Marty more than sixty seconds to decide to send one of his people out of town, particularly to a destination like the Caribbean, a guaranteed red flag when the department's monthly expense sheet went to accounting. They took particular pleasure in using red-felt tipped markers to add question marks and crowd the margins with small questions for expenses that exceeded the cost of a sesame bagel and cream cheese.

"When?" I said. I honestly never expected to be so summarily dispatched, so close to Christmas. It threw all of my plans with Chris and my parents awry. Marty glanced at his watch.

"Now," he said, without looking back up to me.

"You sure?"

"You want to nail the bastards?"

"You don't have to ask me twice."

He reached around and scratched the back of his head. "So get out of here."

I eased the door closed behind me, called travel to arrange the ticket, and then gathered up my bag and coat. I headed outside to flag down a cab. It was snowing lightly, but there was a whipping wind sending tendrils of hair winding around my face like Medusa's. I started drawing up a list.

* Plus side:

   1. Getting a chance to walk in on a meeting of sleazy city officials partying on my tax dollars.

   2. Escaping the freezing air and icy sidewalks of New York during one of its harshest winters.

* Minus side:

   1. On my own for Christmas.

   2. Chris would be on his own.

   3. No presents under the tree.

   4. No Christmas dinner with my parents.

   5. No break from the office to just hang out with Chris and enjoy each other's company.

So the minuses outweighed the pluses, but I had no choice. I turned my thoughts back to the trip and getting away as soon as possible. It had already snowed seven times this winter, and according to the weather report, another storm was on the way. I pulled up the collar of my coat and then started waving again. One cab passed and then another and another, all filled with passengers (how did they get cabs, there were none) or with off-duty signs. Finally I spotted a cab with someone in it slowing down. I strode toward it purposefully, sending the signal to anybody else within a twenty-foot radius that I had staked a claim. New York was like that. You had to strategize to trump the competition. But at that moment, a slick garmento type with greased-back hair had the same idea. But he stopped abruptly. He had seen the puddle. I hadn't. Frozen water splashed up over the front of me like an icy tsunami, spraying the front of my camel's-hair coat.

"Damn," I said, climbing into the cab.

He laughed slightly and turned away, already at work flagging down another cab. I blew him a kiss off my middle finger as we headed downtown.

For the first time since Marty gave me the green light, I realized that it would be the first Christmas that I ever spent alone. And in all the time that Chris and I had been together, we had never been apart for an entire night. Was there any chance that he could just pack up and come with me? I had to work but

I could take time to be with him and explore the island. And then there were the evenings we would have on the beach, or in the hotel, looking out at the water. We got away together so infrequently, and it would give us time to relax and just focus on each other. You couldn't take a relationship for granted, someone in an advice column once said. You had to work at it. We spent so little time working at it because our jobs pulled us in different directions. While neither of us was ready to make any commitments yet, we got along well, we liked the same things, and when we weren't exhausted we were great together in bed. And if things continued to go well, maybe in a couple of years...

Then, of course, I remembered the new ad campaign that he was about to embark on. He'd never be able to get away, how could I imagine it? Holiday or not, if the client wanted to get moving, everyone would be called in, destroying plans and commitments made long in advance.

I became furious with myself for getting so involved in following the story. Who cared if some city workers went to the Caribbean, whether it was ethical or not? There were liars, cheats and employees on the take in every government, everywhere. What was the big deal? Would my work stop that and make everyone become honest? I was one journalist at one paper. What difference could I possibly make in the overall scheme of city government? Was it all so important that I had to give up my Christmas and jeopardize my relationship?

How stupid and shortsighted of me not to first consider how it would affect my personal life. Were my career and my bank account more important than my soul? Where would that kind of thinking ultimately lead—to journalism awards on my bookshelf, while I slept alone in an empty bed wearing frumpy nightgowns?

And even if I did manage to do work that I was proud of, tomorrow was another day and yesterday's newspapers were used to wrap dead fish. There was always a bigger scandal, all you had to do was wait a day. People forgot and the person who was close to indictment today was the same one who was running for office six months later. None of it really made any long-term difference in the world. I looked down at the water stain on my coat as if it was a blight on my character.

At home, I hung my coat up to dry and searched through the back of my closet for summer clothes, another depressing thought. I wish I could say that last year's Gap wardrobe was all neatly folded, but no—clothes were jammed in, and I knew without looking that the white shorts and slacks were stained.

I snatched up one bathing suit, and then a second, a skimpy bikini with a halter top that Chris bought me the weekend we spent in the Hamptons. It was our first weekend alone together and except for afternoons at the beach, the rest of the time was spent in bed in an East Quogue house owned by an art director at Chris's agency. I stood there clinging to the suit, thinking about those days with Chris, until reluctantly I realized what time it was and how little of it I had to pack. I folded the suit and put it in the bag, not sure whether it would still fit.

While packing the rest of my things, I dialed Chris at the office to tell him that I was leaving. I heard the perky voice of the secretary in creative instead.

"He's tied up in a meeting, Jen. Can I give him a *massage?*" Cutesy advertisingspeak.

"Tell him that I had to go down to the Caribbean for a story—it just came up and I—"

"Luck-y!" she said. I guess she heard some hesitation in my voice, because a moment later she said, "Anything else?"

Out of nowhere, tears welled up in my eyes when I thought back to last year and what I was now walking away from. I remembered how we spent hours strolling around from one tree seller to another, searching for the right tree, and then, finally, found one that was too big to fit into a cab so we carried it home, balancing it precariously over our heads. We were going to cook a turkey with corn bread stuffing and make cranberry sauce for Christmas dinner and then drive out to my parents' house in Westchester. Chris didn't cook much, but when he did, it seemed to unlock a whole new domestic part of his personality, and he enjoyed searching through cookbooks, looking for unusual recipes.

Last year, we drove out to Long Island to a turkey farm to pick out a fresh turkey rather than buying a frozen one in our local supermarket, and we bought fresh sage, rosemary and thyme to season it, along with sausage, apples and corn bread for the stuffing.

It was obvious Chris enjoyed being with my parents. They were a normal, middle-class couple who were still in love after forty years of marriage, such a departure from the kind of house that he grew up in with his dysfunctional family. His parents divorced when he was eight, and he grew up going back and forth from his father's place to his mother's, half the time not remembering where his clothes and schoolbooks were. His mother was a shrink, need I say more? They both lived in San Francisco, but other than staying true to the city, everything else about them was perpetually in flux, ranging from their lovers to their phone numbers. Chris rarely visited either of them anymore and except for the annual birthday card, which interestingly enough they both remembered to send, there was little else that physically reminded us that they existed. With me going out of town, he'd be alone for the holiday.

"Tell him I'll miss him for Christmas," I said, hating to share this intimate thought with her. "And tell him that it just won't—"

"Hold, please!" she said like a drill sergeant, suddenly cutting me off. "I have another call."

"Just tell him that I love him and that I'm so sorry things worked out this way." I went on, talking to the void. "It won't seem like Christmas if I'm on my own, without him."

Chapter Seven

The idea of going off on an out-of-town assignment—something I did more often before the column—initially gives me an adrenaline jolt. Getting my reservation for the plane and the hotel, notifying everyone that I'll be away, dashing to the airport to chase a story representing a major city paper, and then writing it according to how I, Jenny George, pursue the facts and set them down for the world to see and for history to record.

Then the true picture emerges. The cab gets enmeshed in a paralyzing thicket of traffic. I teeter-totter to the gate in those fabulous-looking suede heels that I bought, against my better judgment, and sure enough, not only are they starting to pinch, the balls of my feet are starting to burn and feel raw.

I'm hyperventilating. I'm going to miss my flight,

and all of the others for that day are solidly booked, although I haven't checked first class because I'd resort to that only in an emergency. So assuming the gods are looking down at me positively, and I arrive at the airport in time to make the flight, I am now subjected, as is every other passenger, to a security check that makes me fixate on the potential dangers of getting into an aircraft with dozens of strangers.

Don't think I fit the terrorist profile. Not a blue-eyed blonde in Donna Karan slacks and a cashmere sweater from Express, right? Oh, and yes, don't forget the delicate heels. But, hey, you never know, I could be a designer decoy.

I'm pulled apart from the other passengers and a handheld metal detector that reminds me of a billy club is run smoothly over my arms, legs and torso, and unless it can detect pockets of cellulite, and the fact that I'm the only one of my friends who hasn't gone on a low-carb diet, I think I'm clear to go. As usual, of course, I'm thinking of some smart-ass remark to make, but then realize that I had better shut my mouth. These days no one working airport security has a sense of humor.

Following the lead of the person before me, I take off my jacket, then my shoes, put them back on, and get the green light to go. I glance at my watch and take off for the exit gate, arriving just as the doors are about to close.

"WAAAAIIIIITTT," I yell, and it's obvious that

there's a benevolent God because the attendant waves me through. Moments later, I haul my suitcase into the overhead compartment. Then I sit down, belt myself in, and in minutes we're airborne. I close my eyes and then open them in relief when we're soaring above the city.

Only then do I allow myself to think about what Chris told me that morning. He had an appointment with the client and the casting director of his agency to discuss the profile of the girl that they wanted to represent Model Thin. Over the course of the next few days, they were going to start casting calls.

Am I secure, convinced that the man loves me, and unconcerned about the possibility of him being attracted to one of the candidates because he's always been faithful? Get real. I may be reasonably good-looking, and fairly accomplished, but so what?

Do I have alabaster skin?

Am I six feet tall?

Am I model thin?

Do I have perfect cheekbones?

Big pouty lips?

Perfectly straight white teeth, or rather perfect white veneers?

No, and you can be sure that the woman they'd pick would be someone out of his deepest fantasies, not the kind of woman that ordinary guys meet in bars or at their jobs or even see walking on the streets. No, this creature would be some rarefied beauty who spent her days in front of cameras for *Vogue, Bazaar* and *Allure*. This would be a visionary creature who would convince average American women, overweight or not, that they had to head for the supermarket for a drink that would radically change their lives, inviting the kind of happiness and satisfaction that until now they had only dreamed about.

So for no reason other than the fact that she was born with the right face and body, the woman that they picked would be paid enough to retire, for life, after a couple of years of standing in front of cameras and endorsing the useless drink.

How did I feel about that? Cool, accepting, nonchalant? Are you out of your mind? I'm consumed with angst. Why couldn't I just keep my mouth shut? Why, of all names, did I come up with one that used the word MODEL! Couldn't I just have suggested "Makeover Magic" or "Magic Malted"? Then Chris could use cartoon characters or magicians, or any fanciful characters that illustrators could create on the page and then animate. It was a good thing that I was a print journalist rather than a trial lawyer. I'd probably blurt out something that would condemn my client to a life behind bars.

While it wasn't Chris's job to get involved in the casting, I had no doubt that he would. If you were a straight guy and the office was going to be filled with top models between the ages of eighteen and

twenty-five from the city's most prominent modeling agencies, would you go to the deli for lunch or
mosey down to the casting department to check out
the runway show?

I remember a friend who was an editor at the *New
York Times* telling me about the time that Robert
Redford came to the paper for an editorial meeting.
No big deal, right? They were sophisticated people.
The women were liberated. That was until Redford
set foot on West Forty-third Street. Windows were
flung open. Heads were hanging out of them. There
was a stampede to the corridor as the oh-so-sophis-
ticated *feminist* reporters who went gaga wanted to
steal a look at him. Beauty was a magnet.

It's not that anyone would describe Chris as a skirt
chaser. Au contraire, he's pretty laid-back. But he
does have twenty-twenty vision, and he is all male
and at a moment's notice is ready to jump into the
sack. With me out of town now, what was the rush
to come home? So those kind of thoughts haunted
my consciousness for the entire flight. Instead of
using the uninterrupted calm to go over reams of
documents that I had carted along in my shoulder
bag—almost dislocating my shoulder from the
weight—I stared out the window, neurotically chipping away at my nail polish, fantasizing about who
Chris would be going home with and where it
would all lead.

And me? I'd become a prizewinning reporter

sleeping alone with nothing but old newspapers scattered around me, and cartons filled with notebooks with hastily written scribbles everywhere. I'd have plenty of time to write articles, and even books, because my schedule would be wide open without a boyfriend, or husband, or male companionship of any sort.

At the very least, I vowed that although I was destined to spend Christmas alone, I'd get back in time to spend New Year's with Chris. December 31 is always trying for me. I'm not big on celebrations. Maybe because the majority of my New Year's Eves have been spent in the company of girlfriends or family, or just home alone in front of the TV, rather than with the perfect date.

My ideal New Year's? To stay at home alone with a boyfriend, or at most, the two of us with another couple of close friends, sharing a sumptuous dinner of filet mignon or lobster, or maybe bouillabaisse with its heady aroma scenting the house. How depressing to be out at a jam-packed New Year's party with strangers all around you, everyone up at 3:00 a.m., starting to feel sick. It's something that you do to hide your emptiness, like walking alone on an empty street and crying out to fill the void.

Several hours later, I calmed down as I glanced out the window and saw turquoise water all around me. We were descending, getting closer and closer to the tiny island paradise of St. Croix. After a bump, then my sigh of relief, I sat back as we taxied to the airport gate. I stepped down the narrow metal staircase into a warm pool of sunlight and unclouded blue sky toward the arrivals building that's bungalow-size compared to New York's JFK Airport.

Eighty-five degrees at least, the world aglow in late afternoon sunlight. I peeled off my cardigan and then lifted my bags and headed into the terminal. It's hard to keep your mind on work in a place like this when everyone you see is wearing shirts and shorts in bright colors and you see bare, tanned skin instead of cheeks flushed by the cold. The pace of normal life slackens and what's foremost on your mind are things like banana daiquiris and conch fritters and finding a comfortable chair facing the water.

At the front desk of the hotel where I was staying, my initial concern was that someone would recognize me. While I was not going to pretend I was someone else (not ethically acceptable), I wasn't going to advertise my identity either, thus the hair pulled up into a ponytail and the orange aviator glasses. I'd say my name was Jennifer, instead of Jenny, maybe Jennifer Allison, using my middle name and stopping after that. In the gift shop I found a white baseball cap that worked to hide most of my hair. This was not the Jenny George wearing the neat Calvin Klein gabardine blazer that New Yorkers saw twice a week in the thumbnail-size photo in their newspaper.

There are times when it's an advantage not to be statuesque with hip-length hair or the face of a runway model. Right now being the five-foot-six, blue-eyed former cheerleader with standard-issue blond layered hair helped me melt into the crowd.

A porter carried my bag up to a room with a king-size bed. He flung open the dark wooden plantation-style shutters, flooding the room with light and an unending panorama of calm turquoise water. The walls are sponge-painted pale yellow and the bed is covered with a perfectly pressed white linen duvet cover with matching king-size pillowcases. On the desk, opposite the bed, there is a tray holding a cornucopia of fresh pineapple and wedges of mangoes and papaya, surrounded by red and purple berries. He flicked on the bathroom light and I saw that it was the size of a small bedroom, all white marble except for small diamonds of lapis blue. A milk-glass shelf holds a stack of perfectly folded white towels and on top of it a folded white terry bathrobe with the name of the hotel embroidered in gold.

"Is there anything else that you need?" he asked.

Just the perfect man, I was tempted to say, but I didn't because he probably had access to a supply of available men. I tipped him, closed the door and sat on the edge of the bed, running my hand along the fresh, white cover. So here I was, all alone. I reached for the phone and after figuring out the complex equation of outside operator, credit-card number and phone number, I sat back and waited. After eight rings, I hung up. I looked at my watch, it was only six o'clock. Chris was probably still at the office. Another dozen-plus digits or so and the phone finally started to ring again.

Should I ask how the casting went? Would it look as if I was totally insecure and desperate to know what happened? And if I didn't, would he think that I was far away and now oblivious to what his life was like? I was about to hang up when he answered.

"Hey," I said softly. "I'm really sorry that I had to leave without talking to you."

"It's okay Jen, I got your message."

Was he stoned? He sounded even more mellow than usual. Was it the connection?

"So what's going on?" I said. "What are you doing tonight?"

"A few of us are going to Carmine's," he said. Carmine's was a West Side Italian restaurant that served family-size portions of great food. Well, at least, he was in a group. And no doubt he'd come out with enough garlic on his breath to keep werewolves at bay. If he had already found himself a date for the night, he probably wouldn't be taking her to Carmine's.

"Think of me when you have the seafood linguine," I said, instantly craving the jumbo shrimp and the plump steamed mussels, not to mention the nuggets of garlic, the size of peanuts, that were part of every plate.

"Think of me when you're snorkeling."

"Chris…"

"What?"

"I miss you, damn it."

"I miss you too," he said. "I feel abandoned, this really sucks."

"Buy a ticket."

"We're in the middle of planning the campaign right now, Jen, and casting already has someone in mind. The client's thrilled and we're on a tight deadline to go shoot."

"What's the girl like?"

He whistled softly, as though he was entertaining his innermost fantasy. "Pretty amazing."

Was that a migraine aura in front of my eyes, or just the hammering of a major artery in my head? It might even be the first sign of an aneurism, hard to tell.

"So you're moving along," I said, massaging my temples, aware only a moment later of the possible implications of my words.

"Yeah," he said, obviously not picking up on them.

"What's her name?" I asked for no particular reason.

"Bridget," he said.

"Bardot?"

He laughed. "Just Bridget. She doesn't use a last name. I guess it just makes it easier for people to remember her."

"Well, say hello for me," I said breezily.

★ ★ ★

After that I didn't want to go sit by the water or even go near it. What I wanted was a pill that would put me into a long, twilight sleep in the protective cocoon of my king-size bed. The timing of the whole trip was miserable, no matter how you looked at it, and I felt helpless, like someone knowing and dreading the fact that they were watching two trains about to collide. My whole relationship was about to implode. Worse yet was knowing that I was single-handedly responsible. I thought of calling a private investigator to follow Chris to either put my mind at ease or know as soon as possible that our relationship had crash-landed into the gutter.

Bridget, Bridget. Why did the name of a girl who used only one name annoy me beyond my wildest dreams? Probably used just one name because everything else that went with it sounded ridiculous.

Bridget Smith? Bridget Conklin? Bridget Jones? Bridget Wannamaker? It was a stupid name, phony, pretentious. It shouted out that you were a Bardot wanna-be. Maybe I should just drop George and tell everyone that my name was Jennifer. Or Jen, to save newspaper space—a three-letter byline.

I opened my laptop and went to Google. So I was losing it. A moment later, thousands and thousands of mentions came up, including the entire filmography of Bridget Bardot. I scanned through them and soon came to the girl who I assumed would be the new Model Thin face and body.

So she wasn't some neophyte. They had picked a runway model, just twenty-three years old, but already at the top of her game and clearly well known to European fashion designers and Paris *Vogue* along with other popular European magazines. Clearly she would be paid several million to give up her other work and lend herself exclusively to holding up the worthless can of artificially sweetened gunk that contained milk and air held together with emulsifiers, additives, flavoring agents and artificial coloring.

I clicked on a Web site that included models' portfolios, and a moment later, there she was in a skimpy T-shirt that showed a few significant inches of taut midriff over a short denim skirt with a frayed bottom, and pink shearling boots with the wraparound straps hanging open. The next page showed her in a bikini, holding a matching pareu above her head, but the next, full-page picture was the showstopper. It was a Valentine's Day picture done for Victoria's Secret and she was wearing the bra of all bras.

Forget satin, lace, padding, underwire and all the other cleavage enhancers. This one was made from rubies, all linked together with eighteen-carat-gold mesh, a mere five million dollars' worth of support. And her cleavage? Let's just say that Mother Nature didn't shortchange her.

So I was wrong. She didn't need to fantasize

about looking as good as Bardot. She was better than Bardot, reminding me of one of the Estée Lauder models because of her lightly tanned skin, cat-shaped green eyes and full mane of honey-colored hair streaked with gold that made her eyes stand out like radiant tourmalines. She was from Santa Monica, California, and truly looked like a lean, muscular surfer girl. I sat and stared at the face of the girl that Chris would be writing dialogue for. The Model Thin muse who would get American women of all shapes and sizes motivated to buy a useless diet drink so that they could hope to look like her.

I sat on the edge of the bed and stared at the face. How did it help to know the enemy? I closed the laptop and left the room.

The irony is, I was never the jealous or insecure type. Never. Maybe it's because Chris and all the other boyfriends that I've had have never given me reason to be. I've been lucky, I suppose. In every serious relationship that I've been in, both of us have been monogamous, at least while things were good. But this was different. It felt as though the gods had allied themselves against me. I was sent off on a story. It was Christmas. Chris was going to be alone. And as luck would have it, he writes a commercial for a svelte, fabulous girl and the casting director comes through with someone astonishingly beautiful and, according to the little I could glean about her social life, single and available. Could there be a more cat-astrophic sequence of events?

Clearly it was payback time. Had I done something wrong in a previous life? Or this one? It must have been the fact that I had become impossible to live with, high-strung, and unduly hard and demanding on Chris. My job made me mean-spirited, never mind the PMS and the perpetual need to vent at the end of the day. All in all, I had become hard, brittle and simply unlovable. Bridget was his ticket away from me. If she hadn't come along, someone else would have—maybe just a twenty-something secre-tary from his office, or one of the wide-eyed college freshmen that the copywriters and other profession-als sometimes "mentored."

I changed, put on makeup and went down to the bar. A daiquiri would help, intravenously. Food would help too if I could summon the appetite to eat. I walked out to the pool and sat at a bar with a thatched roof. The bartender was using three blenders at once to turn out fruit daiquiris in yellow, white and peach. I wanted to order one of each, but settled for peach and sat back to watch the scene around the pool.

"Here on vacation?" a man asked me. He sat down on the bar stool next to mine. He was dressed in a beige linen suit.

"Well, it is a vacation," I said, half smiling. "What about you?"

"Business," he said, shrugging. I looked over and

noticed the wedding band. Obviously he was traveling alone. Men were rarely so outgoing when they had company.

"What do you do?"

"Movie production," he said, sipping his drink. "Can I buy you a drink?"

I shook my head.

"What kind of movies?"

He smiled, amused. "Major."

"Ah, you must be the one doing the remake of *Beach Party*," I said. "I always hoped they'd make more of those. I was such a big fan of Annette Funicello."

He laughed and stared at me. "The good old days," he said, then leaned closer. "Great eyes... Blue as the water." He didn't blink. "Why won't you let me buy you a drink?"

"I'm fine paying for my own drinks."

"Independent woman. I like that." We sat there looking out at the water not saying anything. Then he turned back to me. "So what do you do?"

"I write."

"About?"

"All kinds of stuff."

"Would I know your name?"

I got up and picked up my drink to take with me. "Maybe," I said, walking away.

I went back to the room slightly tranquilized, and tried on the bikini that Chris had bought me. Dresser drawers are like Dr. Frankenstein's laboratory where mysterious chemical changes take place. Twelve months earlier, the suit was lipstick red. Now it looked heathery red, faded and even misshapen. The gold ring that linked the two cups was slightly bent out of shape. With the needed manipulation, I managed to flatten it. I put the suit on and then tucked in what needed to stay inside. I couldn't help thinking though about how Bridget would look in a bathing suit. Her thighs were long, lean, and firm. I looked down at mine and then reached for my wrap-style cover-up before going down to the pool, all the while dissing myself for not taking the time to buy a tube of thigh-firming cream made with caffeine, or whatever magical ingredient they put in to make cellulite plump up temporarily.

The pool was almost empty, and rather than standing there and inching in, I ducked under the water and began swimming laps, ignoring the soreness in my arms and concentrating on the rhythm of gliding up and back across the pool. Of course, I scolded myself for not taking the time to do all those arm-sculpting exercises on the pages that I had carefully cut out of magazines ("Shapely Arms In Two Weeks Flat") and put inside my dresser drawers. But the more I swam, the calmer I felt, reciting a mantra in my head about self-love and worthiness. Finally, I pulled myself out and sat down on a lounge chair in the sun. A vitamin D bath had to help; I was sorely sun deprived.

Later, I scanned the area. No groups of men talking about escaping New York City. No such luck. I'd have to go back to the bar. It was the only place where I would be able to meet anyone.

It occurred to me that I might be dead wrong either about the city officials being here, or the fact that they really were holding meetings and sharing information that would make their junket totally justifiable. If I was totally off base, my editor wouldn't forget it. Still, I had a hunch and my instincts usually didn't fail me, so I vowed to talk to people like the sparkling, outgoing woman that I wasn't, but could turn on, as needed.

The next thought that panicked me was wondering what Slaid Warren was writing about. In my rush that morning, I had forgotten to read his column. It took a couple of days to get the newspapers in St. Croix. Connecting to the Web wasn't always predictable—so I called my office. I dialed, and after finally reaching the operator, was immediately put on hold. What else was new? If someone was walking a thin line between talking to the press or not, the speed with which they sent you into the black hole of "HOLD" would immediately convince you to hang up and keep the information to yourself, or worse, call another paper.

"Carol, it's Jenny," I said to the metro secretary.

"Hey, wearing SPF 15?" she said.

"No, we're having a torrential downpour," I said,

to please her. "Listen, I was just wondering what's in Warren's column today."

I heard pages turn. Then more pages. "A big heave on corporate donations to the mayor," she said.

I felt myself relaxing. "Great. Nice to know he's not on his way down here."

"No," she said, "and it looks like there's a part two coming next column."

We didn't always write about the same issues, but more often than not if something caught my eye, Slaid was onto it too. The corporate-donation issue was a big one though and I was sure it would keep him at home. Since other reporters on my paper had already been assigned to it, it was one story that I was happy to stay away from. I showered, put on tinted moisturizer, blush, a pale green sleeveless silk dress and silver high-heeled Prada sandals that killed, but I didn't care—they made my legs look long and lean. A five-nine me strutted down to the bar.

Forget how far we've come, a woman sitting by herself on a bar stool beams out PICK-UP BAIT and nothing you do can change that. Reading? It looks ridiculous—you're not at the library, or Starbucks. Blabbing on the phone? Even if you can connect, it's worse than reading. The best you can do is try not to look lonely. Anyway, if you're strategically seated at a resort's main bar long enough, just about everybody will pass by, if not actually stop to have a drink and be part of the scene.

By nine, I recognized three faces that I was hoping to see, confirming my suspicions. They stood together talking and laughing, looking as relaxed as New Yorkers possibly can when they're out of their element. Did I dare try to join them? I decided to hold back. What I'd aim for was to get a table in the dining room near theirs, assuming that they ate in the hotel and didn't go out. I finished my drink and then ordered a Coke to avoid getting totally plastered. Then I tried, for just a few minutes, to decompress and pretend that I was on vacation, rather than chasing a story. I would count my blessings, not dwell on my ill-timed departure. My thoughts went back to Chris. Then they volleyed back and forth between Bridget and him.

Was I so insecure that I was convinced that once my boyfriend was put in the same room as a fashion model, he'd follow her like a dog chasing fresh meat and forget me?

Yes. And worse, he was alone with nowhere to go. And what about the model? Would she be stuck in town as well, without family or friends? The only encouraging thought was that the information I'd found online was outdated and she now had a boyfriend. Or was she gay? That thought raised my spirits considerably.

Thinking of B, because it helped to reduce her to a single initial, even less than her two-vowel name, I remembered the moment when I was telling Chris that Moose didn't made a move on Ellen.

"So let her make a move on him." He wouldn't mind if a girl came on to him, he said. I motioned to the bartender for the check. I looked at my watch. Would he still be out at the restaurant? For some reason I felt as though I had to keep track of him. I signed and started to get up.

"Want to join me for dinner?" I turned to see the movie man from the pool bar. The jacket was gone. He was wearing a black alligator shirt with linen pants. He was tan.

"Sure," I said. Why not?

Chapter Eight

My second drink and it was generous on the rum. I sipped slowly. The fruity tropical drinks go down easy, not to mention how quickly you adapt to the let-your-hair-down world that I was in. I listened to a steel band somewhere out of sight playing "Yellow Bird." They played it so often. Was it the national anthem? My private thoughts were making me laugh out loud, a sure sign that my alcohol level was escalating. I chided myself for not slowing down. I wasn't with Chris. I was out on a story. We toasted, and briefly scanned the menus.

"You're going with the fish," he said, peering up at me from the menu. I stared back at him.

"And you're going with the steak, even though you know if your wife were here she'd tell you to have fish."

"Everyone needs a vacation, right?"

"Vacation from?"

A small smile. "Fish."

His name was Jack Reilly. He was maybe forty-five and headed one of Hollywood's major production companies. Reilly Films was behind at least half of the country's top-grossing films. He wore his company name proudly, stitched on the upper left side of his golf-style shirt like a designer logo, just above an oversize alligator, big enough to swallow the Lacoste-size one. So he had a sense of humor.

"Love the shirt," I said. "Never mind films, you should go into business selling those."

"We sell them at Fred Segal," he said.

"Of course, I should have guessed." Fred Segal was one of L.A.'s trendiest stores, a place where celebrities bought not only makeup, but also clothes ranging from funky to latest designer. It was a place where you might run into Jennifer Aniston and Julia Roberts, or Mary-Kate and Ashley.

"So what are you filming now?" I asked. He off-handedly mentioned a film with Cameron Diaz and Ed Harris, and another with George Clooney and Jennifer Lopez.

"Aren't most of the films these days made in Canada?"

He nodded, rolling his eyes.

"Too many trees, huh?"

"And we'd rather support the U.S. economy." Then he shrugged, brushing aside any further talk of work. The waiter came by. I ordered barbecued lobster. He ordered jerk pork ribs.

"So how long are you staying?" he said, reaching for his drink.

"Just a few days," I said. "I hope to be back before New Year's. You?"

"Same."

"Nice place for you to hold meetings," I said.

"Why not mix business with pleasure?" he said, leaning closer. He sipped his drink, and I waited to see who would look away first. He didn't. "So what happened to your boyfriend? You break up?"

"Sometimes you need to get away by yourself," I said. He nodded knowingly.

"You ever been down here before?"

I shook my head and reached for my drink, playing with the straw.

"You?"

"I used to come down every Christmas. Have you been to Buck Island?" I had heard of it but I'd never been there.

"What do you do there?"

"It's an uninhabited island a mile and a half from here," he said. "Six thousand feet long and half a mile wide. Do you snorkel?"

"Not often."

"You have to go," he said. "It's the perfect place. Buck Island is a national monument. I was going to go tomorrow. Why don't you come along?"

"But you're here on business," I said, pulling back on the reins.

"I can duck away for a while."

I hesitated, feeling as though I was getting backed into a corner. I didn't know him, so why would I go off alone with him? On the other hand, what better way to find out what he was up to.

"Maybe," I said, holding him off. "Let's see how tomorrow goes."

He nodded, and reached over and squeezed my hand. It was a relief when the food was set down between us. I cracked open a red, semicharred lobster claw, revealing a thick tuft of white meat, and dipped it into a pot of melted butter. I wanted to moan with delight. As I got ready to crack the second claw, two city officials who I recognized from their pictures passed by.

Now, with my hair longer than it was in the headshot for my column, and my body a size smaller than when the picture was taken, I was sure that my identity was secure.

"Jack," one of them said, stopping at our table. "We were looking for you earlier." He turned toward me, lowering his eyes momentarily to my cleavage. I was tempted to use the lobster claw as a weapon. "I see you've got a more interesting dinner partner than one of our group," he said, assuming an intimacy that I resented.

Reilly smiled briefly. "Let's have breakfast," he said. "I'll be down around eight." The official patted Reilly on the shoulder. When he walked off, I waited a moment and then turned to him.

"So how is it filming in New York City?" I asked.

"It's a great town."

"It must be a huge undertaking to get your crew settled in and get all the permits you need."

He shrugged, obviously fairly blasé about the production process. "They welcome our business and do their best," he said, obviously not eager to talk with me about it. I decided to stop peppering him with questions and run the risk of turning him off. Instead, we made small talk about my last trip to L.A.—and how I'd probably never consider living there because I'd be consumed with the thought of the next earthquake.

"You have to die of something," Jack said, obviously unperturbed by the specter of natural disasters.

"What makes you nervous? Losses at the box office?"

"Now you're reading my mail," he said, staring back at me.

We made small talk for the rest of the meal. When there was nothing left except lobster shells and rib bones, he signaled for the waiter.

"You can't pass up the dessert," he said. We scanned the menu and looked up simultaneously.

"Chocolate fondant," we said in harmony. The marriage of semisweet chocolate, gobs of heavy cream, butter, sugar, flour and eggs can literally be heart-stopping, but hey, I was out of New York, in a gorgeous place—it was time to indulge. We took turns working our way into it, taking small bites, pretending to be civil. One forkful, then another, then another, until our forks touched in the middle. I put mine down, urging him to have the last bite. He lifted the fork and reached across the table, putting the dessert to my lips. I shook my head.

You're not going to sleep with me, Reilly. He didn't seem to be reading the message. My discomfort made me think of Chris. Not only was I feeling guilty about where our innocent dinner might look as though it was leading, but also, I began to fixate on whether he was in a similar tight situation with—I refused to think of her name.

Perhaps he would go out with her just to get inspired. Just looking at her would make his adrenaline soar and he'd come up with the most arresting campaign that he could put together. On the other hand, maybe her very presence made him freeze up, so that all he could think about when he was with her was getting into her pants.

I looked at Jack and decided to get back to my room before he offered me more than a forkful of cake.

"That was fun, thanks," I said, sliding my chair back. "I have to get back." He looked at me curiously for a minute, narrowing his eyes as if trying to figure out the strategy of an opponent across a poker table, and then simply smiled.

"My pleasure," he said. "I'll see you tomorrow."

I got up and headed for the elevator. Why did it look as though everyone was more at ease than I was? People were sitting at the bar or around small tables as if they had nothing more to worry about than whether they'd stay up for the midnight brunch or not.

As soon as I got back to my room, I kicked off my shoes and jumped on the bed. I reached for the phone and sat with it in my lap for a minute before I dialed. Fortunately, the flowers on the table didn't include a daisy, because at that moment I was in the pathetically helpless state of mind where I would have plucked it, chanting, *He loves me, he loves me not…*

One ring, two…three…four…and then my voice on the answering machine. "You've reached Jen and Chris, we're out right now, please leave us a message." I held the receiver without breathing, and then hung up. I'd rather catch him as he was walking in. It seemed less premeditated to just call instead of leaving a message that would reveal my near hysteria. I'd be cool. I wasn't falling apart because he was involved in an advertising campaign that involved a drop-dead-gorgeous model. So what? I could handle it. I was sophisticated, secure, I had a great job, I'd been around the block.

Why would someone like me be doubled over with *agita?* It didn't matter that I was hours away in the Caribbean and he had the entire apartment to himself. It didn't matter that I would never know if he was fooling around, even in our bed. Not only could he have a one-night stand, he could move her in for a long, leisurely weekend. I would never find out unless he failed to change the sheets and they were scented with her perfume, not to mention anything else.

I stared at the clock. Almost ten. I tried his cell phone but he didn't pick up. I'd wait half an hour and call again. I did. I called at ten-thirty. At eleven. At eleven-thirty. I had become the Stepford girlfriend dialing frantically as though I were programmed to do so. At eight and a half minutes after twelve, he picked up the home phone.

"I didn't wake you, did I?"

"No," Chris said. "I just got in."

I paused for a nanosecond. He got a point for honesty. "Oh…where did you go?"

An equally pregnant pause. "The art director on the account had a party," he said. "Everybody from work went over after we'd finished at Carmine's." Using every molecule of restraint that I could summon, I didn't ask for the guest list.

"Oh," I said, all innocence. "Was it fun?"

"Yeah, it was cool," he said. *Cool* was Chris's favorite word. It drove me crazy. He was a copywriter—

how could he fixate on that sophomoric expression? I suppose I should have taken some comfort in the fact that he didn't say it was *awesome*. Eventually, I just ignored it.

"How are you doing?" Chris asked. "Toughing it out?"

"There are worse places to be," I said. "But I miss you. I'm in this great room with a king-size bed and a mountain of down pillows, not to mention a view of the water, and I'm all by myself."

"I miss you too," he said "Everybody's getting ready to leave for Christmas by the end of the week. If I didn't have to lay the thing out basically on my own, I'd join you."

"When are they shooting?"

"We're trying to set it up for a week from Friday," Chris said. "Bridget wants to go up to her weekend house in Connecticut though, so it all depends on her availability."

"Well, I guess she's a superstar," I said, hoping that I didn't sound snotty. "They probably have to work around her."

"No, actually, she's really down to earth," he said. "I was surprised. She just needs to get away a lot. I guess it's because she's in the limelight so much." That's what I loved about my guy, he was so simpatico.

"Well, I hope it works out," I said. "I know that you probably want to wrap things up." There was a silence for a couple of seconds.

Well?

"Yeah, well, we'll see," Chris said. "Anyway, call me when you know your sked. There's going to be an amazing party here on New Year's. I hope you're back for it."

I immediately felt myself sinking into depression. I thought about New Year's Eve in New York with crowds of people thronging Times Square waiting for the ball to drop. Even though I liked to hunker down, there was so much energy in the air and on the streets. It felt like the whole city was either on its way to or from a party.

"I will," I said, "but I'm just not sure yet what's going on here…but anyway, where's the party?"

"A cool penthouse on Central Park West."

"Nice."

"Yeah," Chris said. "The terrace is all glassed in like a greenhouse, with enormous palm trees everywhere. It's decorated like a movie set with white silk lounges, and there's a Jacuzzi done in green-and-white Moroccan tile big enough for ten people. It's so completely cool," he said. "I've never seen anything like it."

"Sounds amazing. Who lives there?" I said jokingly. "Paris Hilton?"

"Guess again," Chris said.

I hesitated. Other than thinking of Donald Trump, I was coming up dry.

"I give up," I said. "Who?"

"Bridget."

Chapter Nine

It was one of those snowstorms that hit New York with unexpected intensity. In this day and age it's hard to imagine that with all the technology at their disposal, meteorologists can be so off the mark. At most, a light snowfall was predicted—the front was moving down from Canada, but it wasn't supposed to make much of an impact on weather in the city. But by the time it ended, fifteen inches had fallen and another ten were predicted.

When I got over the gleeful feeling that I would be swimming and sunning while my colleagues were trudging over mountains of snow in the Arctic-like cold with their feet buried in heavy boots, it occurred to me that now Chris would have even more time on his hands because many of the employees of his agency lived outside the city and wouldn't be able to make it to work. I was determined to keep thoughts like that at bay and I called the office to see what my competitor was up to.

"What's Slaid writing about?" I asked the news clerk.

"I didn't read the paper yet," she said typically. I heard her thumbing through the pages. Then the rustling stopped.

"He's got a story about the city's growing interest in bringing more business here," she said, unaware of how the news would affect me.

"Shit," I said. "Double shit. Can you e-mail it to me?"

"Our system's down," she said, "and I'm just about to go out to lunch. Can I send it to you in an hour or so?"

"Why should today be different from every other day," I said, thinking of all the system crashes that seemed to happen whenever I was either on deadline or was waiting for some vital information.

"Jen, there's some major system upgrade going on around here for the next two days. We're ready to drag out the typewriters. It's a miracle that the friggin' phones work."

Typical. We were one of the biggest papers in the city, presumably in the communications business, and it was impossible to get a story sent to me. "Well, can you fax the damn thing before you go?"

"I'll try," she said. "What's your fax number?"

I searched through my bag and gave it to her.

"Give me a few minutes," she said.

I headed to the business center to wait by the desk so that the story wouldn't sit there with my name on it. I looked around me. The business center was adjacent to the hotel office. If only I had access to it… As I was waiting, Reilly walked by. Not the most opportune moment to run into him. He opened the glass door and walked in.

"Morning," he said. "How did you sleep?" The question struck me as odd, but I ignored it.

"Like a baby," I said. "I woke up, cried, went back to sleep, and woke up again."

He laughed. "Yeah, same here. We should have gone for a midnight walk on the beach." He shook his head. "Anyway, the offer's still good for snorkeling. I think there's a group of people going over to Buck Island, so we'll have company."

He probably guessed that I wasn't comfortable going off alone with him. Anyway, the problem had taken care of itself. In fact, there was a regularly scheduled tour boat that would drop us off. We'd snorkel for the afternoon and be picked up by three. Reilly left and I turned back to the desk, perfect timing because I was handed the fax. I stuffed it into my purse and went back to my room.

I had to hand it to Slaid. Little got past him. His column started by describing how the city budget needed balancing and how the mayor was making a greater effort to bring in new businesses as well as encouraging others in the arts to use the city's resources to their advantage. It didn't name names, but it was one of Slaid's columns that included the unspoken words "more to come."

At least, from what I could tell, there was no indication that he knew that the mayor's film-office people were in St. Croix. If I got lucky, I'd have that exclusive all to myself. I contemplated calling Slaid and just holding the phone out so that he could hear the soft sounds of a steel band playing "Yellow Bird." But I also knew that I had to move fast; otherwise, even if he was chest high in snow, he'd find a way to join the party, if not sail to Buck Island himself.

But back to me, towel in hand, applying waterproof sunblock and about to embark on my underwater adventure. If you're thinking that I'm an outdoorsy type who enjoys exploring the vast underwater world, you're dead wrong. First, I associate breathing tubes with lying comatose in an ICU unit. And second, as far as covering my eyes with a mask that fogs up and makes eyeliner bleed, my record is about seven minutes.

Still, I was determined to play the part. We met down by the water, and the group boarded a fortytwo-foot catamaran. So much for my concerns about going off alone with Jack in a private boat. Only one face looked familiar. Alex Ryan worked in the mayor's office of film. I remembered seeing his face in an article in *New York Magazine,* discussing scouts for film locations. He was one of a small circle of people in the administration who worked for the mayor before he took office. He was about forty, intense, and bursting with nervous energy and impatience. Judging from the pallor of his skin, I saw him as more of a gym rat than someone who would slow down to snorkel and gasp at natural wonders. I had never met him in person, we had only spoken by phone.

There was little conversation on the boat other than brief chitchat about the extraordinary view, and a few uncharitable asides about the less fortunate, back home, suffering the effects of bitter cold.

"Part of Westchester County lost power because of an ice storm," someone said. We all shook our heads in mock dismay, suppressing tiny gleeful smirks. The only ice here was floating in our drinks. We talked about sailing and sailboats. Of course, Jack had his own sailboat, not to mention a cigarette boat. I guess it went with all the other Hollywood toys that movie types collected.

I closed my eyes, enjoying the breeze against my skin. Physical distance can have a calming effect, or at least give you a long-range perspective, and the more time that I was away, the calmer I felt about Chris. Reilly sat next to me, and even with my eyes closed, I could feel his presence.

What Men Want

Buck Island is one of those extraordinary places beloved by glossy travel magazines that feature it on their covers to evoke paradise. It's a small, perfect, untouched swath of beach with sand as fine as face powder and water that's a startling aquamarine. We anchored at Turtle Beach, on the northwest side of the island, for orientation. The tour company supplied snorkeling equipment and we sorted through to find our sizes. After we were suited up, some of the group took a forty-five-minute lesson. Reilly motioned for me to follow him, and I got a quick refresher course, one-on-one. The hardest part was relaxing and breathing easily with my mouth filled with black rubber, but finally, I got over my initial discomfort underwater.

After everyone was familiar with how to use the gear, we got back on board and headed to the southeast side of the island where there is an underwater trail that's the equivalent of a carefully labeled aquatic museum. While in motion, I learned that the island is built on tectonic plates, and that there are cactus, aloe, and as Jack made a point of pointing out, manchineel trees.

"Don't eat the apples," Reilly said.

"Why?"

"They're poisonous, and so is the whole tree. They say that the sap can blind you if it gets into your eyes." I didn't know trees like that existed, except for remembering something about tree sap that the Native Americans used on the tips of their arrows to make their direct hits lethal. In any case, I'd be hard pressed if I had to survive in the wild. So instead of a picnic under the manchineel trees, we went into the water, staying on the trail and examining brain coral, elkhorn coral, sea fans, sponges, angelfish and parrot fish that flitted by, undeterred by our presence.

It was a living museum of sea life—no wonder people came here from all over to snorkel. I spotted a sea turtle and pointed it out to Reilly. He nodded, taking my hand and leading me out farther. We swam together for almost an hour and then I motioned that I wanted to go back to rest. We swam to shore, and sat at the edge of the water.

"It's an idyllic place," I said. "Thanks for inviting me."

"I was blown away the first time I saw it," he said, as if reliving it. "It's one of the most beautiful beaches in the world."

Probably one of the reasons it was so clean was that it remained uninhabited. Even camping was prohibited. He motioned toward a boat that was approaching.

"They perform wedding ceremonies on board," he said, almost misty-eyed. I stared out at the unending blue water and fantasized about me saying I do under a peach-colored sky at sunset. The only problem was that I couldn't imagine who the groom would be. And now, I was beginning to doubt that the word *wedding* would ever be in my vocabulary. To make things worse, here I was with a married man who wanted nothing more than a quick affair. My self-pity was mixed with self-loathing. It was my own fault. I turned away.

"So how's your marriage?" I asked. He cocked his head to the side and looked off into the distance.

"We've been together for a long time. We lead pretty independent lives."

"Kids?"

"Two—twelve and sixteen. What about you, ever been married?"

I shook my head.

"Boyfriend?"

I nodded, scooping up some sand and letting it run through my fingers. "We live together."

He looked at me for a minute. "But he's not the one," he said, more as a statement than a question.

"Why do you say that?"

He shrugged. "Just a hunch." I was ready to protest, when Alex Ryan came out of the water and walked toward us. He had the body of a man who compensates for his lack of height by spending a gazillion hours lifting weights.

"I'm not interrupting anything, am I?" Alex asked, without waiting for an answer before he flopped down next to us.

Reilly shook his head. "We were just deciding that we were going to stay here and never go back."

"Who's going to make Hollywood's greatest films?"

"The competition," Reilly said dryly.

"There is no competition," Alex said with a sly smile. "Lerner and Dateline send us mugs and flashlight key chains," he said with a snicker. "You're the only class act in town."

I sat there, letting the impact of those words sink in. After being out all morning in the sun, it was almost hard to focus and remember what I was doing here. Lerner was another major film company, and so was Dateline. Was Alex implying that unlike Lerner and Dateline who gave them only cheap advertising toys, Jack was footing the bill for their trip? I was tempted to jump up and start swimming back to the mainland.

I was already plotting what I had to do. Who could I reach from here? I didn't know anyone in the billing office of the hotel, but how about a parent company that owned the hotel? I thought back to the young, blond guy who I had seen when I first arrived. I could try to chat him up, or if that failed, try to get into the office when he was out. An offhand remark was one thing, I needed the documentation.

It was on the tip of my tongue to make a smart remark about a Caribbean junket to draw Alex out, but I decided against it, knowing that I'd end up hanging myself. Reilly was pretty savvy. He'd know if I was fishing. I sat back and pretended to be sunning myself. But Alex didn't say anything else, and soon a colleague of his joined us. The conversation never got any deeper than a discussion of the cost of buying Bacardi in the duty-free shop, the local fish that they hoped to have for dinner and a brief mention of something called ciguatera poisoning that comes from reef fish that feed on toxic algae found in coral-reef areas. Although it usually doesn't kill you, if you get it," Reilly said with a laugh, "they say that you wish you were dead."

Alex shuddered and went on and on about the virtues of the Mediterranean diet, attempting to impress us with his knowledge of monounsaturated fats versus saturated fats and the fishes highest in omega fatty acids. I wanted to ask him how much he knew about the nutritional value of prison food because that might be his next diet.

With just over an hour left before we were to head back, most of the group was eager to spend more time in the water. A few adventurous members suited up and went out deeper with the boat to either snorkle or scuba dive.

Alex said he was joining them—he wanted to explore the depths. I didn't feel comfortable, and I told Reilly to go ahead if he wanted to. He decided to stay behind with me.

So Reilly and I swam together for more of the afternoon until I rose to the surface to take a break. I was heading back to shore when I looked around and saw arms waving madly in the distance. They were followed by calls for help. Everyone else seemed to be in the water, oblivious, and the captain of the boat was nowhere to be seen. I swam out to Reilly, who was underwater, and grabbed him, motioning for him to follow me.

"What is it?" he said, rising to the surface and pulling off his mask. Before I could answer, we heard another call for help and he spun around and started swimming toward the flailing arms. He swam quickly and easily, like someone who had spent summers during college as a lifeguard, even though now, a couple of decades later, his body was thicker and looser than it must have been then. Moments after he reached the swimmer, I saw who it was.

Alex was in a panic, calling out like a scared kid. Reilly swam up next to him and got there before someone from the boat did. He seemed to be talking to him for a few minutes before swimming back to the boat, towing him behind.

I swam out to meet them. "Is he okay?" I asked Reilly.

"Alex saw something with teeth that looked as though he wanted to play tag," Reilly said with a small smile. "He took a swipe at Alex, but he's okay." Alex's face was ashen.

"He was coming after me," he said to no one in particular. "I think he was getting ready to chew me up alive."

We swam around to the boat and boarded, giving Alex a chance to calm down before the others joined us. The captain offered us cold drinks, and Alex sat alone, taking small sips of soda while staring out at the water. Eventually the color came back into his face. Obviously whatever he saw had triggered some kind of primal fear or memory of something frightening that had happened during childhood. He sat looking out, shaking his head back and forth as though he was reliving it.

"I panicked. I couldn't have gotten back without you," he said to Reilly.

"You were okay," Reilly said, belittling his heroism. "You were just a little shaken up. He probably wouldn't have done anything as long as you backed off."

"I don't know what I would have done if you didn't swim out to get me," he said. "I don't think I would have been able to get away. I just froze up. The last time I felt that way I was ten years old and camping in Pennsylvania. We heard a bear or some animal outside our tent."

I looked at Alex and cynic that I am, all I kept thinking was not only had Reilly saved him, but also his heroism would buy him Alex's loyalty, not to mention favorite treatment for the duration. It was a multimillion-dollar rescue. Never mind the pristine beach, my fingers were itching to get back to the keyboard.

Finally, everyone was on board, they took a head

count, and the boat started back to St. Croix. We sat on the padded seats, out in the sunshine, as the rhythm of the water rocked us back and forth. I had always heard that catamarans are notorious for causing seasickness. Now I knew why. Reilly reached for my hand and I couldn't think of a reason not to let him hold it. It was the first time that I had ever held hands with someone who I was investigating. A little voice in my head was admonishing me, but I wasn't sure whose it was—my boyfriend's, my editor's, my own or a Greek chorus of all three.

Chapter Ten

On the pretext of needing to use their computer and go online, I spent a couple of days in the hotel's business office, actually a separate cubicle off the main office. I usually got there at close to twelve o'clock, lunchtime, when I hoped that the office staff would take off not only for lunch but also a siesta. The blond guy I had seen seemed to be in charge of things, but there was another person, a young woman who I guessed was a bookkeeper. As I worked, I noticed that he seemed to go to lunch just after twelve, and she usually left later, closer to twelve-thirty or one. Sometimes she waited for him to come back. I got the hotel's password so that I could log on to the Internet, but I wondered whether there was a way that I could call up the list of guests. I tried various methods of entry, always to be turned down. It was obvious that the machine that I was on didn't allow access to internal hotel information.

But on the third day of my lunchtime visits the blonde went out to lunch and a few minutes later, the young woman picked up her purse and went out too. I looked around. I seemed to be all alone. Did I dare sit in front of her console and try to get into the list of guests? I walked outside. No one seemed to be coming so I slowly walked back in and over to her computer. I studied what was on the computer desktop. There was an icon that said Registration. I clicked on it. It opened to a listing, in alphabetical order, of what looked like the guest list. I scrolled down until I reached the G's and came to my name. There I was. Bingo, I had the guest list. I started to go to the R's to see if Reilly was there too, when suddenly I heard a noise. I closed out the screen and started heading back to the guests' computer.

"Can I help you?" It was the young woman who worked in the office. My heart started to pound.

"I was having trouble with my computer, it just froze," I said quickly. "I thought maybe I could switch over to yours. I was just in the middle of something and I'd hate to have to stop."

She looked at me questioningly for a moment, then shook her head.

"That's the hotel's computer, it's not for guests," she said, shaking her head definitively. "If you want to come back later I can call Robert," she said. "He handles computer problems."

"Mmm, maybe I will," I said. I looked at her and smiled. "Half of these things just seem to resolve themselves if you wait, or just reboot, you know?" She smiled at me politely. I laughed and made my way out the door.

I walked out, aware of my heart beating wildly in my chest. Had she seen me looking at the guest list? I imagined hotel security being called and removing me, handcuffed, from the premises. I hated to do things like that, but what was the alternative? Now I'd have to find some time when they were both finished for the day and the office might be left unguarded. I made my way down to the pool and ordered lunch. I sat outside, watching various guests. None of the film crew turned up, so after lunch, I walked down to the beach, strolling along to see if I could find someone who looked familiar. There was a game of volleyball going on and I asked if I could join.

"Sure," a young man, no more than thirty, said. He was obviously a guest. I played with the group and after a while others joined in. One of them was a member of the mayor's film office who had stopped by when Reilly and I were having dinner. He introduced himself as Tom. I knew that he was Thomas Connelly, the number-two man in the film office. He was on my team, and he was playing the position just behind me. At one point, I ran to hit the ball, and inadvertently fell back, into him.

"Oh, I'm so sorry," I said, just about falling on top of him as we both went down.

I got up first and he struggled to his feet.

"I hope you haven't broken anything," I said, offering my hand, and he got up.

"You're pretty serious about the game," he said, massaging his knee.

We both walked to the sidelines as the game went on without us.

"Can I get you some ice?" I said.

"No, I'll be fine," he said. Then he glanced at me. "You look familiar," he said. "Weren't you sitting with Jack Reilly the other night?"

I nodded.

"How do you know him?"

"We met here," I said. "How do you know him?"

"I work in the film world in New York," Tom said. "Jack's a producer."

"So you're here on business too?"

He nodded. "In a way."

"In a way?" I laughed. "What kind of way?"

"He films in New York and it's my job to help his crew get settled in."

"Oh, give me a job?" I said, pretending to be high on something. "I wish that my company would send me to places like this."

"Who do you work for?"

"Oh, I'm just in publishing," I said.

At that moment, Alex made his way down toward us. Tom waved. "I've got to catch up with my partner," he said. "I hope we see you later."

"Good," I said. "Take care."

Instead of showing up for the Christmas Eve dinner and running into Reilly, I decided to order room service, and then wait until it was dark to go back to the office. The phone rang and I decided not to answer it. When the light went on, indicating there was a message, I dialed the operator to get it. It was Reilly, asking what my plans were for dinner. I didn't call him back. I went out and took a walk on the beach after dinner and thought of how the night would have played out if I were home with Chris, presents under the tree. I put those thoughts aside and when it was close to nine made my way over to the office, avoiding the main area of the hotel lobby. Fortunately the business office was open and I settled in at the guests' computer until I was sure that no one else was around. Close to ten, I got up and tried the door to the rest of the office. It was unlocked and I started to walk in. I hesitated for a moment.

Would my going in set off some kind of silent alarm? I waited for a minute and looked around. It didn't look as though anyone was coming, so I walked in and went to the hotel computer. I clicked on the registration icon and went to the guest list-ing, calling up Jack Reilly and then Alex Ryan. Then I went to my own listing and saw my American Express number next to my name. But interesting that neither Jack nor Alex had numbers next to theirs. Did they pay cash? That would be pretty unlikely. Who travels with several thousand dollars in cash? I clicked on the information under Reilly's name. It listed his room number and several others. I assumed that meant that he was responsible for all of them. I studied the rest of the icons but none of them indicated that they would offer information about guests. I closed the screen and started to leave the office.

Just as I shut the door, I heard a sound behind me. Was someone watching me? Was it just someone passing by? I held my breath for a moment and waited. No one appeared. It was a balmy night and the air seemed to be perfumed with jasmine. I let out my breath and slowly headed for the bar.

But just as I was about to turn the corner, I heard someone behind me. Then a hand reached out and grasped my upper arm.

"Oh," I said, jumping back in surprise.

"Jen?"

I whirled around. "Jack," I said. "What are you doing here?"

He looked at me, surprised. "Just walking by. What are you doing here? I tried to reach you."

"I know," I said, hoping he couldn't hear the way

my heart was pounding. "I had a headache, so I stayed in for a while."

"Better now?" He gazed at me with a questioning look in his eyes.

"Actually, I was just heading back. I guess I had too much sun."

"In the office?"

I looked at him and smiled slightly. Did he see me there? There was no way I could tell.

"I'm obsessed with checking e-mail," I said, wriggling out of his grip. "I'll see you in the morning." I headed toward my room, listening behind me for sounds of him following me. But it was quiet, almost too quiet, and I got into the elevator, relieved when the doors closed behind me. I had my key card in my hand and quickly opened the door, locking it behind me.

The next morning it was Christmas Day and I woke up to a different sky. Hurricane season runs from June through November. So why, in December, was a troubling tropical storm gaining strength at sea and heading our way? The day before, there was only a breeze and the sky was a brilliant blue. Except for the fact that the breeze seemed to be gaining in strength, it was hard to imagine that anything could change. But within twenty-four hours, the blue sky turned charred and overcast.

Reilly called to have breakfast with me but I put

him off. Since I was leaving later in the afternoon, I promised to meet him at the bar to say goodbye before I left for the airport. But now, looking at the sky, I didn't feel like venturing out. I called his room, and fortunately he was there.

"I'm running late," I said. "I have to cancel." He didn't say anything for a minute.

"Stay there, I'll come down," he said.

I hadn't heard from the airline telling me that my flight was canceled, so I packed up quickly, hoping that I could get out before the weather worsened. Years before I had learned that flights in the Caribbean, and the airlines that serve the islands, have their own whimsical way of operating. (Need I remind you that this is the land of, "Don't worry, be happy."?)

I looked out the window and saw flashes of lightning. A horrendous crash followed, as though a building had been knocked to the ground. I went into the bathroom and began fitting every toiletry item I owned into my carry-on bag, as if they were puzzle pieces and each had a particular position where it belonged. I wasn't thrilled about flying on a sunny day, but now with this weather, I tried to steady my hands.

A knock at the door startled me, and then I remembered who it was. I flung it open and went toward Reilly, ready to fall into his arms for protection. But I stopped when I saw him holding out two flutes of champagne. In the midst of this horrendous storm, the image was almost comic.

"The heavens are about to come down and you stroll in to celebrate?"

"This is drinking weather," Reilly said, "not flying weather. Change your plans, for Christ's sake." He handed me a glass and glanced briefly at the sky and then over at the bed. I took a sip and shook my head, placing the drink down on the end table. He leaned over and kissed my cheek and then moved his lips around so that they covered my mouth. I knew I had no more than a second to decide. After that, he'd have me pinned underneath him on the bed. Part of me was ready to abandon myself. Chris didn't want me anymore. No one else did. I was angry and frustrated. I couldn't imagine when I would next get into a situation where basic, raw, uninhibited sex would be in the offing.

Something in me reacted viscerally, however, as though an alarm had been set off to hold me back. In my head there was a vision of Marty sitting in his office with his thick arms folded across his chest, leaning back in his chair like the Lord looking down at me in judgment. I pulled back as though I had picked up some electrical impulse from the office. The Pavlovian journalist learning right from wrong.

"I can't," I said. "You're married and I'm…" I said, letting my voice drop.

"You're what?" he said, shaking his head, obviously growing impatient.

"Involved," I said. He stared at me for a minute.

"Jen…" he started, as if I had made a bad call.

"My cab will be here any minute," I said, stepping farther back from him and looking at my watch. "I've got to go."

"To lost opportunities," he said, reaching for his glass. I couldn't tell if he was high or just acting that way. I toasted back.

"Give me your business card," I said, changing hats. He reached into his back pocket and pulled out a white card from his wallet.

"Call me," he said. "I'm in the city all the time."

I nodded. He started for the door and there was another crash of thunder. Outside, I watched the palm fronds bob back and forth as the wind slapped against them.

"You're not going to get out of here," he said before closing the door. "If the airport closes down, I'll buy you dinner."

"Let's see," I said. Then I put the last few things in my bag, checked out at the front desk and ventured out in the rain, holding my handbag over my head as an umbrella. The cab was waiting, and I settled into the back seat. Rain was pelting the windshield and cars around us were pulling off the road to wait out the downpour.

"The airport?" he said, unsure.

I nodded. "Ummm." He started driving, swerving to avoid flooded areas of the road, and then turned back to look at me.

"Don't think that they can take off in weather like this, miss," he said, shaking his head. As we drove, I watched people on the side of the road. Two young women in loose, flowered dresses and sandals were walking with a large banana leaf that they were holding over their heads. It looked like a scene out of a nineteenth-century photo.

"Wait for me," I said when he pulled up to the airport gate. I gave him an enormous tip. "If they're not taking off, I'll be back in five." I pulled my suitcase out of the open trunk and made my way into the terminal. There was a line of bedraggled-looking travelers in wet clothes up at the front desk. Their dismayed expressions said it all. I waited my turn anyway.

"There's one more flight coming in and then we're closing the airport," the airline rep said.

"Any idea when flights will resume?" I asked.

He held out his hands helplessly. "Listen to the weather report."

I wheeled my bag in the opposite direction and went back outside for another soaking. My cabdriver was waiting with a self-satisfied smile on his face.

"You were right," I said, sinking into the backseat.

I checked back in, but this time I didn't dwell on the size of the bed or the decor. I set up my laptop and tried to connect to do some preliminary research for the story. No luck, of course. Instead, I quickly sketched out a rough outline of what I knew, but there were too many unanswered questions and I turned off the computer, frustrated at how much work was ahead of me. Did I want to go out and run into Reilly again? Where would that lead? Instead, I got into a bathrobe, took a nap, then showered and put on dry clothes. When I finally headed out, it was to the informal café where my chances of running into him were more remote.

Caribbean food can be a welcome change from the New York diet. I started with tomato-based fish chowder and then had golden conch fritters and salad. I read a book while I ate, and after I finished dinner, certain it would be safe, I strolled back to my room, passing the bar area.

There are surprises and then surprises. This one blew me away. Reilly was sitting on a bar stool, nursing what looked like a rum drink. He looked relaxed, smiling. But he wasn't chatting with anyone from the film office. Nor had he latched on to another single female, even though I suspected that he would, as soon as I left. Instead, he was sitting with someone tall, dressed in jeans and a white shirt with the tails hanging out. The hair was dark, long, with bangs swept back off his forehead. Despite the snowstorm in New York, and the tropical storm in St. Croix, there, as relaxed as a tourist at the end of a long vacation, was Slaid Warren.

I was tempted to get a seat somewhere far off in

the distance and just watch the two of them the way I would observe a silent movie to see what I could deduce from their body language. Were he and Reilly old friends? Had Slaid just gotten here and immediately cozied up to him? Had he met Reilly through someone in the film office? I had never seen Slaid in action and I wanted to study him, get a feel for his technique. Most of all I wanted to know how in hell he'd found out that Reilly was down here.

But I lacked the restraint to sit back and observe them until they finally noticed me. I couldn't resist the urge to surprise them. With the stealth of a cat, I crept up behind their backs.

"Well, well, well," I said, patting Slaid and Jack on their backs at the same time. Reilly turned and Slaid spun around, nearly toppling off the bar stool.

"Hello, sweetheart," he said, quickly regaining his composure. At that moment, I regretted my impulsive behavior and began to sweat. Would Slaid introduce me? Would he tell Reilly who I was? To his credit, he seemed to intuit my situation.

"This is Jenny, an old pal from New York," Slaid said. "Sweet-looking, isn't she?"

I wanted to spit.

"We've met," Reilly said, also playing it close to the vest.

Reilly looked at me. "I guess you're stuck here," he said in a slightly superior way. I nodded and turned back to Slaid.

"How did you get here? Did you swim?"

"I hopped the last flight down," he said, obviously delighted that he had managed to slip in before things buttoned down.

"So," I said, wide-eyed, "what brings you here?"

"A piece on storm chasing," Slaid said, pretending to gaze up at the sky.

I raised an eyebrow.

"Naw, Jack's an old acquaintance," he said. "He agreed to be interviewed."

"Really? Can't wait to read your story." I looked at Jack. "You sure that you want to talk to this guy?"

Slaid gave me a dirty look. "I heard that there's a sale in the boutique," he said. "Aren't you girls always excited about shopping for pretty, new clothes?"

"Why, yes, thanks," I said, smiling warmly. "I didn't know about the sale—and while I'm there I'll see if they have any jockstraps for you. Are you still a small?" Reilly threw back his head and laughed.

Slaid looked at me and then at Reilly. "I wouldn't have anything to do with this woman if I were you," he said lazily. "You won't need a jockstrap when she gets finished with you."

Reilly whistled. "This is far better than the cabaret act next door," he said. "So how do you guys know each other?"

"We met for about five minutes, in the lingerie department of Bloomingdale's," Slaid said. "She wears these amazing thong panties in all these hot colors."

I smiled at Slaid and resisted the impulse to slap him. To make matters worse, I could feel my face turning purple. But then a higher power intervened so that Slaid and Reilly couldn't see the color of my face, or even my thong panties if I turned around and mooned them, which I felt like doing, because at that very moment there was blackness. The storm had caused the island to lose power. All around us, it was pitch-black. The only illumination came from tiny flickers of candlelight on the cocktail tables.

"Blackout," someone yelled, and people seemed to be scurrying around frantically to find their way. The bartenders and waiters snapped into action, lighting more candles and reaching for hurricane lamps to pass out. This was nothing unusual for them.

"I guess the only thing to do is turn in for the night," I said. "Don't lose your way in the dark."

I blew a kiss at Reilly and Slaid and then with the help of the flashlight on my key chain that I bought after New York had a summer blackout, I fumbled my way around to the staircase and carefully felt my way along the corridor until I found my room. I thought about the storm, and the sudden appearance of Slaid. If I didn't know better, I would have assumed that one of Reilly's screenwriters had a hand in plotting this story. The only hitch was it might not come out exactly the way Reilly wanted it to.

Chapter Eleven

Sometimes it feels as though half of my social life is conducted on the phone because everyone has such hectic schedules and can't find the time to actually get together. One of my very favorite New Yorker cartoons, in fact, shows a man in his office on the phone, saying something to the effect: "The sixteenth isn't good for you? How about never, is never good for you?"

Ellen and I don't actually see each other more than about once a month, but we talk almost every day. Her day starts at the gym. She goes when it's still dark, whatever time that is, then she's in the studio at about the time I'm heading for the shower. But evenings, before she goes to sleep—about the time that I'm unwinding from work—we try to talk and catch up.

"I didn't wake you, did I?" I said from my hotel room in St. Croix.

She yawned. "I just got off the phone with Moose. Did you know that his real name is Larry?"

"No wonder he prefers Moose."

"Exactly," Ellen said. "Anyway, he invited me to visit him, but I don't know."

"What a great escape," I said. "Why are you nervous?"

"He seems pretty intense," she said. "I don't know how it'll work out, not to mention the sleeping arrangements."

"You can always stay at the Lake Placid Lodge," I said. It was a posh Adirondack-style resort with great food and rooms furnished with whimsical Adirondack furniture made by local artists. But what I remembered most wasn't the expansive lake view or the posh decor. It was the enormous fireplace just off the dining room, where I found an elegant silver basket that contained all the makings of s'mores.

If you've never been a camper, you may have never heard of them. Think melted toasted marshmallows heaped onto chunks of milk-chocolate bars so that the chocolate softens before you sandwich it between graham crackers. How did it get the name s'mores? Because you have one and you want Some More.

But Ellen wasn't thinking about those kinds of desserts.

"The Lake Placid Lodge wasn't what he had in mind," she said.

"Have you been seeing much of him?" Unfortunately, since I had to go out of town, Chris never got the concert tickets and the four of us never had a chance to go out together again.

"I saw him a couple of other times," Ellen said.

"And?"

"We got along well," she said.

"And?"

"The answer to your next question is no, but we might have if it wasn't a workday and I didn't have to get up at five...."

"So why are you unsure of whether to go?"

"I have too much on my plate every day, to get sidetracked now." She paused. "And he lives such a different life," she said with the emphasis on *life*.

"You're afraid."

"Of what?" she said indignantly.

I didn't answer.

"Okay, maybe," she peeped.

Ellen was engaged years before. At the last minute, after all the plans for the wedding at the Plaza Hotel were in place, and the flowers were ordered, along with her Vera Wang gown, good old Eric pulled out. Rumor had it that he was conflicted all along and ran back to his old girlfriend, who, it turned out, later married someone else. One of the gossip columns picked up on it, making it all that much more excruciating for Ellen to bear. All of us pride ourselves on being astute judges of character, until someone comes along and acts inexplicably, totally blowing our confidence.

"You can't walk away from life because one relationship went sour," I said softly. She didn't say anything so I brought up Reilly and then Slaid.

"Slaid?"

"The one and only," I said.

"How the hell did he get there with that storm?"

"God sent a plane," I said. "Anyway, he's here, and the first thing I saw was him hunkering down with Jack Reilly."

"Why do I remember some gossip item about Reilly?"

"What do you mean?"

"I can't remember. Something, maybe 'Page Six' in the *Post*."

"I think I may go back to the bar and look for Reilly," I said.

I was in my bathrobe, but I got dressed again. The rain was still pelting the windows and it felt as though the entire building was swaying under the force of the wind. I grabbed my flashlight and slipped into my sandals. I would have been better off barefoot, but whatever.

I didn't get too far. There was a strange noise at my door. Was someone trying to get in? I was probably imagining it. Maybe someone was just making his way along the corridor and grabbed my door-knob to steady himself. But then I heard the sound of an electronic key card being slipped into the lock. And then again. Then the doorknob was being turned impatiently even though the lock hadn't opened. I looked around frantically, running to grab the heavy leather-bound book with hotel informa-tion off the desk. I held it over my head, ready to use it as a murder weapon.

Would Reilly have the nerve to try to get into my room? What an incredibly sleazy thing to do. Then again maybe it was someone trying to break in, tak-ing advantage of the blackout. Whenever there was chaos, there were lootings, robberies. I positioned my-self then yanked the door open so that at least I had the advantage of surprise. I slammed down the book.

"UGG..."

A body fell at my feet.

"Christ, what the hell are you trying to do?" said a male voice.

I peered at the shadowy form on the floor. "Slaid?" What are you doing?"

"I thought I was trying to get into my goddamn room. I didn't realize I had to carry an assault weapon to protect myself," he said, getting to his feet.

"What's your room number?" I said, not believ-ing him.

"409."

I pointed to the door opposite mine. "That's you," I said, annoyed. "I'm 408."

"So I made a mistake. It's pitch-black. You didn't have to act like a pit bull," he said as he stood up.

We stood there staring at each other, and then started to laugh. He shook his head.

"I'm sorry," I said, "really...I thought you were Reilly."

"Reilly? He wouldn't have broken in, he would have had a duplicate key."

"You're probably right." I stood there for another minute. "Well, good night," I said, starting to close the door.

"Wait," he said, rubbing his shoulder where I had slammed it. "I think I need a drink, or at least something to eat. Do you want to join me?" He smirked. "I'll even let you pay."

I stared at him for a minute. "Sure," I said, feeling guilty.

We left the room and followed the corridor until we reached the staircase and slowly made our way down. I knew that there wouldn't be any food at the bar, so I led the way to the coffee shop, where a waitress was cleaning up by candlelight. She made it fairly clear that she would have preferred that we hadn't shown up. Still, she offered us salad and hard-boiled eggs that had been in the refrigerator that was slowly warming and lit the candle in the hurricane lamp that was between us.

"I can't remember the last time I left New York for a story," Slaid said, continuing to rub the spot where I had swatted him. I pulled his shirt to the side and saw that the spot was already turning purple. I took a piece of ice from my drink and wrapped it in a napkin, handing it to him. He took it and held it over the spot, obviously wincing from the pain.

"Neither can I."

"You're writing a story?" he said, laughing as though he was high on something.

"Yes," I said, starting to laugh too. "If I ever get out of this place."

"It's so surreal. We're on one of the most gorgeous islands in the Caribbean and it gets hit by a tropical storm and then I almost get beaten to death." He shook his head. "Who would have thunk it? Still," he said, pushing his plate back from the table. "I'm not leaving this place until I have a tan, I mean it. The hell with the story. Even if that means tying up Jenny George so that she doesn't scoop me."

"It's so ridiculous," I said, "isn't it? I mean, what's the big deal if your story runs first or mine does?"

"I know," he said, nodding in complete agreement. "We get so caught up in the newspaper-competition bullshit. I mean, who really cares?" We talked about his first days on the paper and lessons that he'd learned from a more senior writer.

"I actually asked him if he ever made up a quote," Slaid said, obviously amused by how naive he was when he started out. "He looked at me aghast. 'Make up a quote? Are you kidding? You NEVER, EVER do that…that's awful.' He looked down, paused for a minute then looked back at me sternly. 'You make up a whole person.'"

I told him about the time that I wrote a freelance travel article and picked up a quote directly from a government-issued press release, something I later learned a more experienced reporter would never do. My editor—who didn't know where I got the quote—asked me to ask the source another question. I tried to reach him, to no avail. Why? He had died years before. Needless to say, I quickly substituted a quote from a live person and learned only to quote people I had actually spoken to.

We sat there for an hour, maybe more, until the waitress started mopping the floor under our feet, and the restaurant was scented with Lestoil.

"Uh, I think she wants us to leave," I said.

"Guess so," he laughed.

He walked me back to my room and when we got to the door, the flashlight's batteries went dead. It was starting to feel like a reenactment of *RENT*.

"Good night," he said, squeezing my hand.

"Good luck with your story," I said.

"Yes, the story," he said. "Right, I kind of forgot about that."

I let myself back in the room and then waited until I heard his door close. I sat on the edge of the bed and started to undress. Then, suddenly, the lamp next to my bed went on. The power was back. I looked at my watch. It was almost 4:00 a.m. I opened my door slowly and made my way back to the business office for a last look.

The world was remade when I woke up at eleven o'clock. An arresting blue sky had taken the place of darkness, rain and shrieking wind. I forgot where I was for a moment and then things came into focus. The airport had probably opened hours ago. Instinctively, I called the main desk and asked for Slaid's room. I didn't know what his schedule was, but if he was leaving today, maybe we could fly out together. I hated to fly alone, at least his company would make the time go faster. She paused for a moment.

"He checked out," the receptionist said.

"Checked out? Do you know when?"

There was silence for a minute. "It looks like five forty-five," she said.

I called the airport and found out that not only had flights resumed hours earlier, but they were now all booked, except for an 8:00 p.m. flight.

"You should be happy that we have a seat left," the agent told me. "People were lining up this morning to get the first flight out."

The hell with it, I wouldn't call him. He obviously stayed up all night to make sure he got on the plane. He didn't waste time thinking about me though. As the minutes ticked by, it occurred to me that he'd probably planned the whole thing so that I'd go to sleep late and miss the morning plane. Maybe he'd even dropped something in my drink. I wouldn't put it past him. There I was, stuck in St. Croix while he was deep at work at his office.

After brooding for most of the afternoon, I couldn't keep my hands off the phone any longer and tried to take a few deep calming breaths before I bared my fangs.

"I guess you got yourself a really quick tan," I said, calling his office number.

"Mmm, I have sensitive skin."

"We get so caught up in the newspaper-competition bullshit," I said mockingly, repeating his words from the night before. "I mean, who really cares?"

"You're getting a little carried away, Jen. It wasn't like—"

"Wasn't like what? You could have called bright and early to let me know that the airport was open and planes were taking off. But no, you were nice enough to let me sleep in."

"Look, I would have—"

"Warren, go screw yourself," I said, slamming down the phone, surprised by the sudden surge of anger in my gut. If he was any kind of friend, he would have made sure that I was up too. If it wasn't for his late-night visit, I would have been up bright and early. I couldn't remember the last time I slept until eleven. But with the storm, and my exhaustion... And in keeping with his slimy character, he slipped out on the first flight so that he was guaranteed to scoop me.

To distract myself, I called Chris. I knew he would be at the office, but I hoped I wouldn't be catching him at a bad time.

"Hey," he said. "Where are you?"

I explained about the flight and the storm.

"Glad you're okay. I didn't even know about the storm." That was typical Chris—he rarely kept up with the news, let alone the weather. Why pay attention when your job was to reinvent reality?

"I'll see you at the apartment later. I've got to run to a meeting."

Sometimes reaching someone you need to talk to who's too busy to talk is worse than getting their voice mail. They may not mean it, but it sends a signal that they've got more important things to do than stop and talk to you. I should be the last one to feel that way considering that I bark at anyone who calls me on deadline. Still, I was particularly sensitive now when it came to Chris. I hung up the phone and headed out to walk on the beach.

Debris was scattered everywhere, and it looked as if the hotel staff was all out doing their best to clean things up. I walked up and down the length of the beach, tucking some seashells into my pocket. I lifted up a toppled lounge chair and sat in the sun, staring out at the water. There was such a rough edge to the day, it was almost more appealing than when things were perfectly manicured. Regardless of your stress level, the view of an endless body of water, the same one that generations and generations of vacationers before you have stared out at, can serve to remind you that in the scheme of things, you and your problems fade into insignificance.

Did I really care that Slaid might beat me on this story? Yes and no. I was more concerned about getting the whole story and getting it right than getting it into the paper before he did. How many times had journalists cut corners to file a story before another paper or news station, only to realize that they didn't get the story quite right, and went ahead when they should have showed restraint.

But what really infuriated me was the way Slaid had played me. First he was the true friend, the colleague, not a competitor. He established a rapport, put me at ease. Was there even a sparkle of interest in his eye? And then *bam!,* when my guard was down, he made sure that I'd be too exhausted to get up and leave while he skipped off to the airport to be at his desk before I opened my eyes.

What I really wanted to know was how hard he had leaned on Reilly and what he had gotten from him. Reilly would never have offered that he was footing the bill for the entire group. At best, he would have fabricated some convoluted story. Of course, Slaid had ways of getting information though, and maybe if he confronted Reilly with what he'd found, Reilly wouldn't be able to deny it.

Taking another approach, Slaid had dated his fair share of models and celebrities. Maybe he knew Reilly from the L.A.–New York party scene or from movie premiers or restaurant openings. Maybe they even had girlfriends in common. In any case, it was useful to make a friend out of someone who was a member of the press, especially someone of Slaid's professional stature. Instant access when you needed to get out a message. Hollywood hotshots got off on publicity and recognition. Sometimes they talked too much.

I had a few hours before I left. It would be my last chance to talk to Reilly. I went back to my room and changed and put on makeup. It was lunchtime, he'd probably be somewhere near the restaurant. Sure enough, he was sitting at an outdoor table, this time alone. It looked as though he had just finished eating.

"Hey, movie man," I said. "Want company?" He gestured for me to sit down.

"When do you leave?"

"At eight."

"Your pal Warren took off at the crack of dawn, I think," he said. He looked at me for confirmation.

"I wouldn't know," I said. I turned in early, well, early in the morning. I don't think he believed me.

"I have to ask you something," I said, trying a last-ditch approach.

"Shoot."

"Did you bring the crew from the film office down here?"

"Is this Jenny George the reporter talking now?" He leaned into me and smiled in a way that crinkled the corners of his eyes. His recognition unsettled me for a minute, but it shouldn't have. How could I possibly have thought that he didn't know who I was?

"That's the only Jenny George there is," I said, softly using the same approach to him that he'd tried to use on me. The truth was, I really didn't want to hurt him. I had grown to like him, even feel sorry for him in some inexplicable way. Still, I didn't want to hear something that was off the record.

"Here's my idea. Why don't we spend the afternoon together getting to know each other…and I'll tell you more about the way I do business."

I looked at Reilly for a long minute and he held my eyes. Was this some kind of sexual quid pro quo?

"I need to know more about the way you do business right now," I said, looking at him levelly, keeping my voice as calm as Ellen's when she was on the air. "Slaid Warren's working on his column about you and the film office and so am I. I want to get it right, Jack, and I don't want to hurt you. I like you, I really do."

"I'm flying back to New York in three hours. Do

you want to join me?" I thought about flying back on his Learjet instead of being scrunched up in economy class. Hard to say no, however, it was a suicidal career move. I shook my head. He got up and pushed his chair in.

"You write what you have to, newspaper lady," he said softly. "But I hope you get it right, because if you don't," he added, leaning so close to me that our lips almost brushed, "I'm going to sue the pants off you and your paper, and the only thing that you'll have to cover yourself up with will be the First Amendment." He started to walk away, but I called him back.

"Jack."

He turned and waited.

"Someone in hotel administration showed me your bill."

He looked surprised for a minute and then recovered. "When all else fails, use the bluff," he said.

I gave him an enigmatic smile and walked the other way.

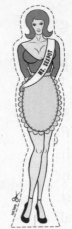

Chapter Twelve

I got home close to midnight. Chris was sitting up in bed with the TV on Jay Leno. I dropped my bag and went over to him.

"Hey, stranger," I said. "I missed you."

"Missed you too," he said, hugging me. I couldn't help glancing around the room. Except for a shirt on the floor and the unmade bed, things weren't tossed all over the place the way I expected to find them.

Quickly, I ran to my closet and pulled out the present. He looked at it and then got his gift from under the bed. Without speaking we unwrapped the boxes. He stared at the bag for a moment and didn't say anything. "Thanks," he said awkwardly. "It's great."

I tore open the red paper on his gift and lifted the

cover of the box. I lifted out a blue cashmere cardigan. "It's beautiful," I said. "I love it."

I stared around the room. "You even cleaned up for my return," I said. "I'm impressed."

He shrugged. "I've been too busy to even spend any time here. Things were all screwed up at the office…" He shrugged and didn't go on. I was too exhausted to press him. I washed up and got into bed next to him and he flicked off the TV. Almost instinctually, I turned to him. We had been apart for almost a week. I wanted to devour him. He kissed me back briefly and then shook his head.

"Jen, I'm sorry," he said. "I'm just so bummed, I've got to go to sleep." I didn't remember Chris ever turning me down. I was usually the one pleading exhaustion or depression.

"Sure," I said. I rolled over and tried to sleep, but I was more consumed with listening to the sound of his breathing to see if he would go right to sleep or lie awake. I knew that I would. He got moody occasionally, who didn't? But this wasn't like him. I decided not to dwell on it. Maybe it was just the pressure of the job getting to him. And at any rate, the last thing I wanted right now—as selfish as it seemed—was to be thinking about problems with Chris. I had enough on my head with the way the story was going—or wasn't. If I started dwelling on what was going wrong in our relationship, it would sap me of all the energy I needed at work.

Of course, Chris went right to sleep, while most of the night I lay there imagining every possible scenario of what was ahead, not only between me and Chris, but also with Slaid's upcoming column. He would beat me, I'd play catch-up and my reporting would look weak and lackluster to my colleagues. My ego was on the line. I had to do better than him, especially after the way he fled St. Croix, leaving me behind, oblivious.

I tried to relax by fixating on mind-numbing things like the arrangement of the furniture in the room. That usually helped. But now, it felt as though my brain was prisoner to some drug that kept me alert.

In the early-morning light, I felt calmer, more secure. I wouldn't worry last night to death. I'd act as though nothing had happened. Maybe I had just overreacted. So I was away. His life went on and he was entitled to be depressed if things at work weren't going well. There was a lot of pressure to get the copy right, and he was the lead writer on the ad campaign. Maybe being on his own made things worse because he had no one else to share the burden with. It was a new day, we'd start over.

When I woke up, I wanted Chris even more. We needed to make love, reconnect with each other. But I rolled over and found his side of the bed empty. I got up and went into the living room. Was he up having coffee? Then I saw the note on the table:

Jen: Had to rush off to an early meeting. See you tonight. C

With the column to write, I couldn't let my mind wander. Years before, I had a boyfriend who taught me a very useful skill—compartmentalizing.

"I don't worry about things until I have to," he said. I remember looking back at him quizzically.

"You don't stop worrying," he said. "You just decide that right now the time's not right and you tell yourself that you'll worry about that issue more productively when it is."

It sounded completely ridiculous at the time, impossible to follow. I was sure that there was no way I'd be able to rigidly control my thinking. Eventually, however, with everything I had to do each day, I found out that I could do it, even had to do it. It was a survival mechanism that prevented me from frittering away my time unproductively. In fact, it was like establishing a mental to-do list that brought some order to a chaotic mind.

Slaid's column came out the day after I got back. I grabbed the newspaper and opened to his page, scanning the column. At first I thought that I was reading the wrong one. It had nothing to do with Reilly or the movie business. The headline threw me:

Who Doesn't Have Time to Volunteer?

WHAT? A column about a new program to get more New Yorkers involved in volunteering? That came out of left field. Now I was consumed with wondering what he had or didn't have, and why he was holding off writing about Reilly and the city.

No matter what he knew, my ace in the hole, however, were those few words out of Alex's mouth that told me all I needed to know. *"There is no competition. Lerner and Dateline send mugs and flashlight key chains. You're the only class act in town."* My version of things, written from the point of view of a firsthand observer, would be stronger than anything that he could come up with.

As it turned out, there would be mystery on both ends. I didn't have time to finish my column either, so I used one unrelated to Reilly as well—on library budget cuts.

"Libraries, huh?" he laughed.

I didn't say anything, and anyway, I was still seething.

"You decided to save his ass?"

"Not exactly," I said, a trifle patronizing. I didn't go on to explain.

"We both know he's finished, he hung himself," Slaid said.

"First of all, it's 'hanged' himself," I said impatiently. "Pictures are hung, people are hanged."

"I'm—"

"Don't…" I said.

"So how did things with you and Reilly end up?"

"Oh please," I said, hanging up.

The truth was, Jack Reilly was right—I tried to bluff him, and he caught me. I knew what the story was, it was just that I couldn't prove it—yet. The hotel computer confirmed what I suspected, but that wasn't something I could put into the column. And if I rushed to print something and made a mistake, I would open myself and the paper to a big fat lawsuit. I knew that he had paid for the trip, I just had to find the proof. What I really needed was his American Express bill, a receipt if he had paid cash, or some other explanation why he didn't need to provide a credit card number and neither did the others from the mayor's film office.

I sat at my desk, getting depressed. How would I possibly get what I needed? When all else fails, go back to the clips, read over everything that has been done on the person you're interested in a second time to see if there is something that you missed.

I noticed that one of our reporters did a story on Reilly a few years before that I hadn't read. It mentioned the names of several executives in the company. I noted them down and then checked to see whether they still worked for him. It turned out that a former vice president—Keith Watson—left to open his own production house and that he had an office in New York as well as L.A. He had had differences with Reilly, one of the stories said. That immediately opened up a window of opportunity. Disgruntled employees make good sources, but first I checked to see which, if any, of our reporters might have interviewed him. Keith's name came up in a financial story. His office told me that he was out of town, so I called the reporter who wrote the story and she gave me his cell number. I called, and he agreed to talk to me.

We had an amicable meeting a few days later in his office in Turtle Bay, a largely residential part of Manhattan that's close to the East River. Keith's company wasn't in Reilly's league—he had only been on his own for a few years. He briefly mentioned differences with Reilly, but he didn't specify what they were. At the end of our discussion, I popped the question.

"Keith, I don't want to put you in an uncomfortable position or anything—but I know how expensive and overwhelming it can be to film in New York City and that the mayor is eager to attract new business here." I paused, and he nodded.

"But what I'm concerned about is whether city officials may have crossed the line and are either using taxpayers' money to treat themselves to lavish trips to invite business here or whether Reilly's trying to get favors by paying for Caribbean trips taken by city officials."

Keith smiled. "Jen, I don't know whether he did or not...not that it wouldn't be his style to buy his way...but I can give you the phone number of the girl who used to be his secretary, maybe she can help."

"Used to be?"

"She left," he said.

"Why should she talk to me?"

"Well..." He paused. "She didn't leave under the most opportune circumstances."

"Oh?"

"You didn't hear it from me," he said, "but rumor has it that she was sleeping with him, and rumor has it that things didn't end all that well."

"I'd love her phone number," I said, sitting up straight. He pressed a few keys on his keyboard and then wrote down the number on a piece of paper and slid it across the desk to me.

I left the office feeling as though someone had given me the winning lottery numbers. I had no real reason to get so excited, but my sixth sense told me that I had hit pay dirt.

Hell has no wrath like a woman scorned, and Marilyn Morgan was living proof. We met at the bar of the W Hotel in Union Square, and I had no trouble finding her, the tall redhead with pale skin and cat green eyes among a sea of far more ordinary-looking women.

"Mmm, I worked for Jack in L.A. for almost a year, and then I moved here," she said, sipping a gin and tonic and leaving a dark lipstick stain on the white straw. It didn't take much imagination to picture her next to Reilly. In her fitted black suit with short flared skirt that showed her long legs, she looked like the type that was used to getting in and out of black limos, not to mention black negligees. We chatted about how she got the job—through an actress friend who knew Reilly—and what he was like to work for.

"Cool…charming…testosterone driven. Easy to get along with unless you got on his bad side."

"So why did you leave?" I asked.

She looked at me quizzically for a moment, then smiled benignly as if she had made the decision to destroy him.

"Jack and I had an affair for almost five months," she said in a deep, kind of smoky voice. "It began less than a month after I started working for him. We were together a lot, worked late, had dinner together all the time, often with clients, but sometimes not…." She looked off, as if reliving it. "It was almost inevitable. After a month or two, he realized how helpful I could be to the company, and he started taking me on business trips with him out of town." She held her head up high. "On the rare occasions when his wife would leave town, he would stay over at my place." She described the places they went—the upscale West Coast resorts, the Hawaiian Islands and the Caribbean.

"It was like a honeymoon. Plus I got paid well and he taught me the business. Eventually I became more of a partner than an assistant, going out with directors, actors and actresses on my own and bringing in considerable business." She dropped names along the way of superstars with whom she had worked in film. But then her face clouded over and she looked down at the table.

"Then at some point, I had the feeling that he'd met someone else," she said. "I thought it was a young actress who he wanted to lure for an upcoming film.... He kept asking me to find out where she was and how he could reach her." She shrugged. "He was always looking to sleep with women he'd just met...I think he needed the validation."

"When was that?"

"Sometime in March of last year."

I held back asking who it was, not wanting to stop her recollection. "I didn't find out at the time, but he started traveling more on his own, not always explaining where he was going and who he was with. Once he told me he would be in Europe and needed me to stay behind." She pushed a stray lock of hair back off her face.

"Then one day, someone called up saying that she had to cancel dinner. She had a soft, breathy voice—familiar to me, but I couldn't place it. I asked her to leave her name, but all she gave me was her first name. She said he'd know who it was. I realized instantly that she was Jack's latest conquest." I watched her shaking around the ice cubes in her drink, reliving the moment. I waited for her to go on.

"I confronted him, but of course he denied it." She ran her hand back through her hair. "Things started to go downhill between us. I wanted him to leave his wife but he wouldn't. Eventually, he said he thought it would be best if I left the company. He offered to give me half a year's salary."

"I guess he has a habit of trying to buy what he wants."

"But he couldn't buy me," she said, shaking her head emphatically. "And not only did I leave on my own, I called his wife and had lunch with her."

I nodded as if we were members of a secret sorority. We talked about cheating men and meting out punishment, and finally, I segued to the Caribbean trip.

Marilyn nodded. "He does that all the time," she said. I did my best to stay cool.

"You wouldn't by any chance have any documentation at this point, would you?"

"I kept copies of everything," Marilyn said, flashing a quick smile that then disappeared. "Jack taught me that. The paper trail. And when things started to go downhill between us, I wanted all the ammunition that I could get."

I swallowed involuntarily. She made Glenn Close's character in *Fatal Attraction* look tame.

"Would you show me what you have?"

She studied me for a minute. "Things are put away," she said.

"Can you get to them?"

She was silent for a moment. "It really puts me in an awkward position."

I nodded as if I totally understood while at the same time knowing I had a matter of minutes to try to convince her. "I'll leave your name out of it," I said. "And—"

"Jack will know that the information came from me."

"There were other people in the office, weren't there?"

She nodded. "But no one who had direct access, the way I did."

"But he can't prove that you gave me anything. You stopped working for him." She looked at me as though she was mulling it over.

"Why should you protect *him*?"

"I'll make you copies of what you need."

I nodded slowly. "That would really help."

We headed out of the hotel together. She was going downtown, and I was headed home. I zeroed in on the heart of the story.

"This past week he was in the Caribbean with

people from the city's office of film. While you worked for him did he ever take executives on junkets like that?"

"He's part owner of a hotel in St Croix," she said. "He puts people up there all the time."

"So there's no bill?"

She gave me a coy smile. "Not unless you need one." I looked at her questioningly.

"We made up bogus bills to make it look like the people he was entertaining paid their own way," she said, then raised her hand to flag down a cab. I nodded.

"I'll call you tomorrow," I said, "and I appreciate all your help." She climbed into a cab that pulled up, and slammed the door.

As it was about to leave, she looked up at me. "Did you sleep with him?"

I shook my head. "No."

"Too bad," she laughed. "He's very good."

I walked uptown to go over my meeting with Marilyn. I relished the thought of putting together the story. If Marilyn came through, I had all I needed to write the story opening both Reilly and the city officials to indictments on federal charges of bribery and fraud. I walked along the streets with thoughts of Reilly and Marilyn swirling around my head.

Someone, somewhere, must have done a study on how long the average extramarital affair lasts before one of the parties loses interest and the relationship ends, often with disastrous consequences. Then there was Reilly's wife. She knew about his dalliances but stuck with him. Women like that always fascinated me. Didn't it matter to them? Were the extracurricular activities of their husbands of no consequence to what went on between them? Or did they care but hang on at any cost to preserve the relationship?

Chris and I have a favorite Japanese restaurant in the Village where you take your shoes off at the door and then sit on the floor in front of low tables. I called Chris at work and we agreed to meet at the restaurant after work. He was anxious to get away, he said. I took that as a good sign.

In the meantime, I went back to the office and started to make more calls on the story. The phone rang at six-thirty. I assumed that it would be Chris, saying that he was packing up.

"So what big splash are you going to make on Thursday?"

"Hand in your resignation, Warren, you're dead in the water."

The signature laugh. "And here I thought that I had to watch out for you," he said.

"I can't imagine why."

"It must be your innocent and vulnerable veneer. Now I know what a ruse it is."

"It's done with smoke and mirrors," I said. Then, don't ask me why, I sighed and turned serious.

"Do you ever stay up at night worrying about the consequences of ruining people's reputations, not to mention their careers?" There was silence on the line for a minute. I wasn't usually one to talk about issues like that with someone from a rival paper, but I suppose that the tension of the story was getting to me, and lately I felt as though Chris was around less and less and that we seemed to have so few intimate conversations.

Slaid must have heard something in my voice, because he became serious too. "A couple of years ago, I wrote a column about a guy who was an egregious expense-account cheat." He waited as though collecting himself. I heard him take a deep breath. "The day after the story came out, he took the elevator up to the thirty-first floor roof of his Sutton Place apartment building—and jumped."

I closed my eyes and didn't say anything for a few seconds. "I remember," I said finally. "That's hard to live with."

"It threw me. I even thought of resigning. But even things like that can't stop us from doing what we do."

"I know." Neither of us said anything, but I heard him take in a labored breath.

"Bye," I said softly. "Thanks." We both hung up, almost at the same moment. I think it was the first serious phone conversation that we ever had.

I packed up my bag and left to meet Chris, making a stop in the ladies' room to wash and put on lipstick and eyeliner. I felt a flutter of nervousness, as though I were going out on a date with someone for the first time. I thought about those dating services where you spent something like fifteen minutes with each new man or woman, and I wondered what Chris would think of me if we were meeting for the first time. There was no doubt what he or any other guy would think of Bridget. First impressions die hard.

But now, we would be sitting face-to-face. We'd have time to talk about his work, the campaign, even the model at the center of it. I'd give him a chance to open up, and by the time we were having green-tea ice cream, I hoped that I'd know whether or not on Sunday I needed to reach for the *New York Times* real estate section before any other to search for a new place to live.

Chapter Thirteen

One reason to go up to the Adirondacks in the dead of winter is to ski. Another is to go to the winter carnival, which takes place every year and lasts for about ten days, starting in early February in Saranac Lake, New York.

As I was heading out for dinner, Ellen phoned to say she had gone up to Saranac Lake to join Moose, who was working with local townspeople to plan the carnival. He told her about the barbecue in the snow, and they decided to have their own outdoor barbecue after they went snowshoeing. I told her that I couldn't think of anything more romantic.

"It is," Ellen said, "especially after you've gone snowshoeing and burned a thousand calories a minute, and you're starving and tired and just want to cuddle up after you've had the most scrumptious dinner you can imagine."

Then she told me about his house.

"I expected a rustic cave, but it was just the opposite." She described a large open living room with dark, heavy furniture that he made himself. "And remember those red-and-black jackets that lumbermen wear that we had in college?"

I did.

"He used blankets like that for upholstery fabric. The couch is covered with red-and-black plaid, and the chairs are solid red. The bedroom, which is in the back of the house, has a picture window that opens to the woods." I imagined that it was like sleeping in a Ralph Lauren diorama.

"He should clone the house and go into business," I said, reminded of a man I had once met who gave up a successful career in advertising in Chicago to move down to Virgin Gorda, another gemlike Caribbean island. But instead of finding an existing house, or even building one of his own, he opted for a more unusual, alfresco habitat, and moved his furniture into a hollowed rock formation, like a large open crater facing out to sea. Everyone who came to his cave home was so enchanted that they wanted places like that for themselves, and eventually, he created open rock-homes for them. Little did he know that when he left Chicago to more or less retire, he would start a new career as a real estate developer.

"Moose is amazingly innovative," Ellen said. "He fascinates me."

"So you're getting along well?"

"It's good," she said. "Very good."

I wondered whether he was in touch with Chris at all. I doubted it though. They seemed to talk pretty infrequently, except when Moose took a rare trip into the city.

"How long are you staying?" I asked. She was up in the mountains in a winter paradise, and I was riding the M15 bus on a congested avenue with cars honking, sirens screaming in the background and the woman next to me coughing with bronchitis or pneumonia. I turned my head the other way, reminding myself to wash my hands the moment I got in the door.

"Just until Monday," Ellen said. "I have to get back. How are things with you and Chris?"

I didn't want to broadcast the "relationship report" to riders on the bus. "Call me when you're back," I said. "I'll tell you whether to make up the guest room."

He got there before I did, and was talking on the cell with one hand while sipping saki from a small square wooden cup with the other. He held up the cup as a wave, and I slipped out of my shoes at the front of the restaurant and then padded over to the table and sat down on the floor. He looked cute in a worn red T-shirt and jeans.

"Next week's not good," he said into the phone. "We're going down to the Keys to shoot."

I shook my head. I had just gotten back from the Caribbean, and now he was heading off?

"I do want to see your portfolio," he said. "But I'm just jammed up right now." He rolled his eyes. "Yeah," he said, and then hung up.

"Hi, sorry. It's all hitting the fan." He leaned over and kissed my cheek.

"You left so early," I said. "I missed you."

"They're really cracking the whip on us with this campaign," he said. "They want it on the air ASAP so that by summer Model Thin will be a household word."

I let that sink in for a minute. The real question was whether Bridget was becoming a household word—in *my* household.

"I'm glad it's working out," I said, feigning earnestness. "I didn't realize what I helped you give birth to." He stared at me for a minute and then burst out laughing. I started laughing too and felt this enormous sense of release. The old Chris was back and I leaned over and hugged him.

"I'm starving," I said. "Should we get the humongo bento box?" For some reason, that struck us as funny too, and I felt all my uncertainties disappear as we spent the rest of the dinner talking about the agency, my trip, Reilly, and then Marilyn.

"You think she'll come through?"

"Yes, why, don't you?"

"Sounds like she likes to play games."

"I guess that's why she and Reilly got along, but now I think she wants revenge and enjoys the thought of destroying him."

He shook his head. "Scary broad," he said. He looked off into the distance and then back at me.

"Did he come on to you?" he asked.

I looked at him, surprised. "Sort of."

"And?"

"And what?" I said.

"Did you sleep with him?"

"No," I said indignantly.

"Did you want to?"

"What is this, Twenty Questions? I was there to do a story and that was it. I'm living with you, remember?" He nodded and didn't say anything else. We finished the last two pieces of sushi—"you have it, no you have it"—and then walked out and headed uptown. He held my hand, and we didn't talk much. Bridget didn't come up, and I got the feeling that he wasn't thinking about her. I was out with the old Chris, and for the first time in a week, I felt relaxed and confident, picking things up where I had left them before I was away.

When we got back to the house, Chris filled the bathtub for me. We had some lavender oil that we picked up one day when we wandered into an aromatherapy store and wanted to buy some scented massage cream. He sprinkled a few drops of it under the running water and soon the aroma wafted through the house. I soaked in the hot bath and felt my tight muscles uncoiling. Chris came into the bathroom, sitting on the side of the tub, and we talked intimately the way we used to about friends, jobs, the news and even future vacations. I got out and he wrapped me in a large bath towel, giving me a massage as he rubbed me dry, then he picked me up and carried me to bed.

We took our time making love and I tried to fight off images that flashed through my brain of him with Bridget. "Did you sleep with her," I wanted to ask him, just to be reassured. But I didn't dare.

"I missed you," I said. "So much."

"Mmm," he whispered back. "Me too."

We seemed to connect on a deeper level, as if our bodies were rejoined after a long separation. Or maybe it had just been so long that my body was hurting from denial and wanted to melt into his. Finally, we fell asleep, cocooned in the lavender-scented air. When the jarring alarm went off at seven, I stayed in bed, dozing, while he got up and showered. He woke me up with a kiss at eight.

"I'm pushing off to the office," he said. "I've got a day."

"What time's the party?" I said, remembering that tonight was New Year's Eve.

"Not sure, about nine, I guess." He kissed me and walked out.

Eventually, I got up and headed for the shower. I turned on the water and let it run over me for a few minutes to wake me up. I reached for the soap and then noticed something that I had failed to see the night before. His bottle of Calvin Klein body wash that had sat on the edge of the bathtub unopened for as long as I could remember was now open. About a third of it was gone. The strange thing was, I never remembered smelling it on him.

It was a small thing, maybe something completely meaningless, still I was obsessed with it. Chris didn't use scented body wash, never had, so why would he start now? I couldn't help thinking of those articles entitled "Signs That He's Having an Affair" that asked questions like:

- Is he suddenly taking a greater interest in his looks?
- Is he showing unusual interest in buying new clothes?
- Has he recently joined a gym?

All morning long, the damn bottle of Obsession permeated my consciousness like a gnat that is flying in your space, refusing to leave you alone. What was I supposed to do, call him up at work in the middle of everything going on with his campaign and ask him why the bottle of body wash was suddenly open? And not only why it was open, but what it signified. Who are you scenting yourself for, and why in hell did you suddenly change your tastes and opt for body wash? It became a subject of cosmic importance to me and it overrode every other concern that I had.

Then a darker, more upsetting thought eclipsed that one. What if it wasn't Chris who'd opened the bottle? What if Bridget had stayed over, slept in our bed and used it in the shower? Or what if they'd showered together and washed each other with it? Clearly, he didn't feel as though he had to cover his tracks. He could have thrown the thing out—destroying the evidence, if he'd even thought of that. But no, it was there on the edge of the bathtub where it had sat for six months, maybe eight. It had come in a gift box that he got from a photographer's rep, I think, after he recommended that his agency start using the photographer.

Clearly, I knew that he never used cologne and that was fine with me. While I liked just the barest hint of scent on the side of his neck, there was nothing worse than a choking veil of it, especially if it was early morning. I spent far too much time thinking about the body wash, to the point of almost crossing the street against the light, forcing a car to come

to a screeching halt. The driver gave me a murder-
ous look. I imagined the headline:

Newspaper Columnist Maimed
Obsessing on Obsession.

I had to stop obsessing. In the world of newspapers, you never get a break and I had work to do.
Things don't close down for holidays. There's no
midwinter break for Christmas or New Year's. And
not only don't they slow down, when everyone else
is home with their families, or off skiing in Colorado, news is scarce, the paper is short staffed and
short of copy, putting the pressure on reporters who
aren't away to come up with stories.

I was determined to focus on filing the story on
Reilly and the mayor's film office as soon as I could.
I called Marilyn, and we agreed to meet at her apartment. She had the documentation, she said, and she
had already made copies for me. She lived in a high-
rise on the Upper East Side that featured a gargan-
tuan marble lobby with a fountain in the middle. The
only thing missing was violin music and perhaps a
gondola. I took the elevator up to the twenty-fifth
floor and she stood waiting with the door open,
greeting me as though we were old friends. I started
to take off my shoes when I saw the white carpet,
but she waved and said it wasn't necessary. From the
wall of windows, I could see all the way east to the

river and the Fifty-ninth Street bridge, across to Queens, and up north to the Bronx. It was like being in a plane.

"What a fabulous place," I said. She smiled and offered me a seat on the sleek, contemporary white leather couch. She took a bottle of Chardonnay from a silver wine bucket filled with ice and poured a glass for me and then one for herself. I was glad she didn't propose a toast. I took a sip, reluctant to drink when I had a long night ahead of me, and then put the drink aside. Finally, we turned our attention to a leopard file box filled with papers that sat on the black granite coffee table in front of us.

"Do you pay news sources?" she said with an enigmatic half smile. I looked back at her for a moment. Was I going to lose this treasure trove before my eyes? She didn't look like a girl who needed money, but maybe this was why.

"We don't," I said. "It's just the policy of the paper. If you were talking to a reporter from a supermarket tabloid, things might be different." Then I gave her a half smile. "I'd be happy to take you out for lunch or dinner—"

"Just thought I'd give it a try," she said. She sat down on the couch in front of the box and for the next hour I looked at copies of hotel bills going back over several years made out in the names of city officials—both familiar and not—who Jack had entertained at the hotel in the hope of buying benefits beyond the usual largesse of the city. I filled several envelopes with the papers. I had what I needed, now I wanted to leave, before she changed her mind.

"Where are you working now?" I asked.

"I'm starting my own production company," Marilyn said. "Downtown."

"How's it going?"

"Okay," she said. "It just takes time to build contacts and get recognition."

"Do you ever see Jack anymore?"

"No," she said. "He's several lovers down the line by now."

"Thanks for everything," I said, feeling as though I wanted to give her a hug. "I'll call you." As I was about to go out the door, I turned back to her.

"I never did ask, but I wondered who the actress was that he started seeing that broke up your relationship?"

She looked at me and smiled. "Someone a lot younger than Jack," she said. "A starlet he could lead by the nose because she knew that he was her ticket to fame." She hesitated. "Do you know Kelly Cartwright?"

It was one of those déjà vu moments when all the pieces of a puzzle seem to come together as if they were pulled by a magnetic force. Six degrees of separation. I tried to hide my surprise and just nodded.

"Mmm, I saw her in *Living on the Edge*," I said, now

finally remembering the name of the movie. Marilyn rolled her eyes.

"She really was pretty pathetic," I said, shaking my head in agreement.

"Everyone thought so except one or two studio heads," Marilyn said. "And I never understood Jack's attraction. Maybe he was hoping that she could get him out of his midlife-crisis doldrums." I laughed as though I were her ally. Maybe hanging around Slaid Warren—even for a short time—had taught me how to pretend to be everyone's best friend and confidante.

Of course, that was the cynical take. In truth, what I really learned was that he was a good reporter because he was genuinely good at relating to people. They weren't just news sources, they were human beings.

I looked back at Marilyn as I picked up my coat to leave. I hoped that she would give me the same amount of credit.

Chapter Fourteen

It had gotten dark outside and instead of walking, I got into a cab. It was only seven and it was unusually quiet on the street. People had come home early to get ready for the night. I thought of calling Ellen, but then decided that I didn't want to have the conversation in a cab. Just my luck the driver would be a young acting student who knew Kelly Cartwright, or worse, knew Jack Reilly. I held the envelopes close to my chest and when we got to the front of my building, I paid and almost dashed into the front door.

I was home before Chris and I grabbed a yogurt. Was I hungry or just nervous? I got into the shower and spent far too much time blowing out my hair. Chris came home after eight, probably the last one to leave the office. Needless to say, I wasn't looking forward to the party. Last New Year's Eve came only two weeks after we met. He took me to a nearby French restaurant and then we went home and stayed in, watching TV. Just after twelve we made love. I wished we could spend the night the same way this year.

"Wouldn't it be fun to order caviar or something and stay in?" I said, throwing out the thought.

"It's probably going to be an unbelievably cool party," he said, obviously all geared up to go. "Very A-list," he said, only half joking.

"I bet she was up all night cooking," I said. He looked at me and laughed.

"Yeah, the naked chef," he said. I hesitated, then laughed too. I went into the bedroom and stared into my closet. Nothing very A-list hanging in front of me. Then again how could I compete with women who were best friends with the designers and could pick out what they wanted? I was tempted to grab jeans.

I ended up with a simple black sleeveless Jil Sander dress that I had picked up on sale. I put on high heels. Chris whistled when he saw me. I tried to hold on to that. Uncharacteristically, he had on a black cashmere pullover that I didn't recognize and black gabardine slacks.

"Very GQish," I said. He flexed his biceps. Since we knew we'd have no shot at finding a cab, we ended up taking the bus along with other overdressed partygoers who had also given up on finding taxis.

I don't know too many people who live on Fifth Avenue, but Bridget's building had someone at the door to open it, a second just to accept packages, a third to hand out mail, and then a fourth to operate the manned elevator that takes you up to your floor.

As the elevator rose higher and higher, the music got louder and louder. "She hired a band," Chris said, and when the bronze doors separated on her private floor, I saw it off in the distance, out on the glassed-in terrace.

But first overall impression: a paradise of twinkling lights. Candles everywhere, hundreds of them, like tiny glinting snowflakes in the darkness. The view was magical, overlooking Central Park with the outline of West Side high-rises in the distance. I recognized people from Chris's ad agency, saw an assortment of faces who looked as though they'd just come off the runway, and then there was an eclectic assortment of fashion types wearing everything from Goth getups with torn mesh stockings, to prim cardigan sets and neat Kate Spade accessories. We went through the usual rounds of hugs, pretentious European cheek kisses (why both sides?), all the while trying to find out where the hostess was hiding herself.

"So where's Bridget?" Chris asked finally. Fabulous-looking girls everywhere, but no sign of her.

"She's inside, putting on the bra," someone said. "It just got here."

"What's that supposed to mean?" I asked, swiping a glass of champagne from the tray of a passing waiter.

Chris laughed. "She said she wanted to wear the ruby Victoria's Secret bra if Harry Winston let her. But I thought she was kidding."

"Oh, that sounds appropriate," I said, remembering the picture of her that I had seen from the catalog. Suddenly I felt like a nun about to chastise a student whose skirt was too short.

"What about thong panties?" I said, unable to rein myself in. "I hope Harry made her one to match." But Chris didn't hear me because at that moment, Bridget walked into the room, and his head swiveled as though he were a puppet and she was controlling the strings.

I'm happy to report that Harry came through for her. Glittering rubies embedded in gold mesh sprinkled with diamonds covered her breasts (well, almost). Even the straps were studded with stones. To match, she was wearing a red satin miniskirt and red metallic sandals with heels that I guessed to be about four inches high. These had a row of rubies (not real, I think) going up the front of the foot and around the ankle. She wore bright red lipstick and little other makeup. Conversation came to a standstill in the room. She waved at Chris.

"Holy Christ," he said to her. "You look fucking fabulous." He walked up to her and dipped her backward, planting a kiss on her lips.

"This is so crazy, don't you think?" she said, working hard at trying to look unsure of how she looked. "I can't believe they let me wear it," she murmured to him. She motioned to three men behind her in black suits, Harry Winston bodyguards who kept the bra company whenever it was out on the road. Chris whispered something else close to her ear that I couldn't make out because at that moment, everyone in the room flocked around her, either to get a closer look at the bra, or what was under it, depending on whether they were female or male.

"Do you believe her?" Chris said, stepping back and turning his head toward me for an instant. Then it must have occurred to him that he hadn't introduced me, because he called out to Bridget.

"Bridget, this is Jen," he said. But by that time, she had taken off to talk to someone else on the other side of the room.

He shrugged. "Sorry, she's off."

"Mmm," I said in reply, not sure whether to just back off and leave or slap him for forgetting that he had come to the party with his girlfriend, his lover, someone who he had been living with for an entire year.

The effect that Bridget had on Chris seemed to be echoed all over the room in the eyes of every other male who was invited to the party. The women, on the other hand, all turned into motes of dust, invisible as they floated into oblivion in various places in the apartment. Even among the other models Bridget was the cover girl, the star, standing six-one in her shoes, with her faceted rubies shining in the glow of the candles. The president of Chris's agency arrived and quickly made his way over to her, ushering her into an empty room as though they had urgent business. They stayed there for a while, chatting, but I'm not sure because as long as she was out of my line of sight, I felt a sense of relief.

When they finally emerged, the band began to play louder. Bridget grabbed a glass of champagne and tilted her head back, drinking it down quickly. She started to dance by herself, and soon there was a crowd around her, clapping and egging her on. She shimmied, breasts forward, so that all eyes were on her chest. Finally, someone tall who looked like a male model joined her and they began to slow dance as the music changed.

As Chris talked to different people from his agency, I made my way around the apartment, peeking into the black-granite kitchen, then walking on into the dining room where there was a white marble table with steel chairs around it. The master bedroom must have originally been two rooms because it had to be at least forty feet. There was a queen-size platform bed with a white leather headboard and ledge around it. Over it was a white mink throw. The wooden floor was pickled white.

"It's an amazing place," said another girl who was

also on a self-guided tour. "But then again what else would you expect when your father owns a shipping company."

"So she can afford to buy the bra," I said.

She laughed. "Ordinarily, I don't think she wears underwear. At least that's what I read in *InStyle.*"

"Well, I don't blame her. I gave up underwear after my ruby panties started giving me an awful wedgie."

She took a step closer to me and looked around. "You won't believe what I heard."

Did I really want to know? "What did you hear?" I asked finally.

"She died her hair red," she said, pointing downward, "to match the outfit."

"Cool," I said, trying groupiespeak. All I could think of was finding the little white tin of Excedrin that I always carried for moments like this, when one of those tension headaches presses down on your scalp like a vise. I walked out into the living room to look for Chris. He was talking to the art director on the account.

"Cool party, huh?" he said, putting his arm around my waist.

I raised my glass of champagne instead of answering. It was five minutes to twelve. Everyone was moving toward the terrace to watch the fireworks that would erupt in Central Park at twelve o'clock. Bridget seemed to be floating around the room from the arms of one man to another, each of them eager to whisper secrets in her ear. She was clearly in the bag. Wherever I was in the room, I could hear her peals of laughter. What could possibly be that funny?

Arnie Harris was Chris's main art director on the account, and Chris was standing with him talking about their upcoming trip to the Florida Keys. Arnie knew the area, he said, he had spent several winter vacations down there and was talking about the best beaches to use for locations. Then he talked about an old hotel where the crew could stay.

"I can't wait to get some sun," Chris said. I looked at him and felt my blood start roiling. I had invited him again and again, but all he said was no. Now, suddenly, he was craving sunshine?

"I'm going to sleep out on the beach," Bridget said, entering our group at that moment. She slipped one arm around Arnie's waist and the other around Chris and pulled them close to her. A moment later, someone began counting down to twelve o'clock.

"Ten, nine, eight, seven, six, five, four, three, two, one...HAPPY NEW YEAR!"

"Happy New Year, Chrissy," she said, first throwing her arms around Chris and pressing herself up to him as she kissed him.

"Happy New Year," Chris said, hugging her back then letting go as she moved on to hug and kiss Arnie. Chris turned to me.

"Happy New Year, Jen," he said, hugging me, and

then briefly kissing my lips. I kissed him back, wiping away the red streak that she had left on the side of his lips.

Despite the fact that I have little interest in television, I got home and dropped my pounds of paperwork on the kitchen table, and then sat in front of it to watch the news on New York One. It was two days after New Year's. Why was I still tired? After the headlines, I held the remote and just channel surfed in my TV stupor. I'd wait for Chris and watch an old movie, or some dumb reality show. I'd relax and veg out. But I stopped the clicking when I came to *Entertainment Tonight.* Actually, I think I held my breath. Who was being interviewed? None other than Miss First Name Only.

"Bridget," the exuberant airhead who was interviewing her yelled out like a cheerleader shouting out the name of the winning team. "You've just been given a ten-million-dollar contract from Cache drinks to be the poster girl for Model Thin. How does it feel?"

She offered a guilty smile momentarily and then brightened.

"I'm excited. I think it's such a fabulous drink—it tastes just like a malted, but the great news is it contains only one hundred and eighty calories and can replace one or two entire meals every day, so it's an easy and fabulous way to lose weight."

Ugh, she sounded as though she were reciting something she had memorized for a midterm exam.

"But you obviously don't seem to have that problem," the airhead giggled. Clearly, the marketing people at Cache had prepped Bridget.

"All of us have weight issues. I certainly never got a free ride when it came to maintaining my body. I was even pudgy as a kid" (pudgy? she looked anorexic), "so as I got older, I really started watching what I ate. Plus, now I exercise."

"Really, what do you do?"

"I run almost every morning, and when I'm in California or Hawaii I surf."

She surfed? Could I hate her any more?

"If I didn't, I'd definitely be heavier," she said, tossing back her blond mane. She slumped forward, thrusting her pelvis out, then crossed her legs. The camera zoomed down to give the audience a closer view of her body. In her pencil-thin white jeans and pink stiletto heels, it was a laugh to imagine her having weight issues, other than those relating to brain size.

"Bridget, we're running out of time," the airhead went on. "But I'd like to ask you just one more question. Bridget nodded. "Is there any truth to the rumors about you and a certain Hollywood leading man?" she asked with a knowing wink.

"I really like to keep my personal life personal," Bridget said. "But for the record, no. The only one in my life isn't a celebrity at all. That's all I'll say."

"Thanks, Bridget," the airhead said, applauding and gesturing for the audience to join her. "She's gorgeous, isn't she?" Bridget smiled to show her white Chiclet teeth and then got up and pranced off the stage.

"The face and figure of Model Thin," the interviewer said, continuing to applaud as if the broad had done something to warrant applause instead of merely being born lucky.

I wanted to heave. Probably as close as she ever got to the awful, sickly-sweet chalky drink—that tasted like a combination of malted and barium-enema fluid—was holding a can as she endorsed the checks. If I ever had a reason to despise ad agencies…

It was hard to resist calling Chris to tell him that he had better find a more meaningful job or I couldn't sustain our relationship. On the other hand, he made a hefty salary and almost every month or so a headhunter called him to see how happy he was and whether he might consider moving to another agency. The next thought I had was wondering how Chris would have reacted to the absurd interview. Usually we were on the same page when it came to shooting down bullshit. But in this case, I was sure his judgment might be a bit clouded.

I didn't have to imagine for long. A minute later the phone rang, and I told him that his Model Thin model had been interviewed on *Entertainment Tonight*.

"Yeah, I went with her," he said.

"You *went* with her?"

"Yeah, a bunch of us went over to keep her company. We hung out in the greenroom when she was on," he said. "It was such a goof, wasn't it? We nearly fell over when they asked her about her weight issues," he said. "I never saw a girl who could eat cheeseburgers and fries the way she does and never gain an ounce."

"Really?" I said. "How lucky." Then, changing the subject, I asked the question that was really on my mind. "So who's she seeing?"

"What do you mean?" He sounded confused, uncomprehending. Suddenly the award-winning copywriter had trouble with the English language?

"Who's her *boyfriend*. She said that she was seeing someone who wasn't a celebrity. I thought I'd pass it on to the gossip column."

"Oh…I don't know. She's probably got all these guys circling her like bees around honey."

"Oh," I said. I didn't like the image, but then again, ever since the New Year's Eve party, there wasn't much about Bridget that I liked, except for her Fifth Avenue building. In fact, we hadn't even talked about the party after it was over. It was obvious to Chris that I didn't have the same great time that he did.

"Anyway, I'm not going to make it home for dinner. I've got to stick around—we're having a brainstorming session on where to go with the campaign."

So much for the dinner out with him that I had been counting on. "I'll see you later then," I said. I flipped the TV back on and sank deeper into the couch. I went from one station to another, wondering whether I'd be treated to another model interview. Finally, I shut off the set and spread the papers from Marilyn over the kitchen table, making notes about who Reilly's guests were and how many of them were repeat offenders. There was a slip of paper with Alex's name, showing that he had been to the resort three times. Then I looked back at city records documenting which films had been made in New York. Interestingly enough, Reilly's company was a major player, except during the administration of the previous mayor. It didn't look as if any of his staff had been visitors to Reilly's hotel.

By the time I finished working, it was ten and Chris wasn't back. At eleven, I went to bed. He usually wasn't this late, but it had happened before. Sometimes he went out for drinks with people from the office after a meeting. It helped him unwind. I had been in bed for about fifteen minutes when I heard his key in the door. I lay there, quiet. Should I ask him how the brainstorming session went, or just pretend to be asleep?

"Hey," I said, rolling over. "How did it go?"

"Okay," he said. He went into the bathroom and I heard the toilet flush and then the water go on.

After he'd showered, he got into bed next to me. I turned toward him. "Long hours, huh?"

"Yeah." Almost involuntarily I reached over and started rubbing the back of his neck. He lay there without moving. Not even a slight sound or moan of pleasure. Very slowly, I dropped my hand and ran it over his body. I touched him softly, lightly, which was usually all it took. But this time, there was no reaction.

"Are you okay?" I asked softly.

He exhaled. "Yeah, I guess." I wanted to ask him what was wrong, but I didn't. Like a wife who knows that hearing the truth is the beginning of the end, I kissed him and then turned over and went to sleep. In the morning, I was the one to get out of bed at the crack of dawn to go to the office. I only realized when I got there that I had put a suit jacket over a skirt that didn't match. My outfit was a mess, but at least it matched my mind.

Chapter Fifteen

My column was going to set off alarms. People from the mayor's office had gone to the Caribbean to talk business with Hollywood hotshots, taking free flights and staying at a five-star resort. It would be hard to calculate just how lavishly they thanked producers like Reilly with contracts, perks and freebies, including free car rentals—compared to other studio heads who didn't entertain them—and in the face of budget cuts for police and firefighters. But most of all, they were breaking the law and living—well, the life of Reilly! I laughed out loud.

Not only were they guests of Reilly's, they had bogus receipts to prove that they had paid when they hadn't. It would be a lot harder to point a finger at city officials who had used city funds to pay for their trips, even if the whole thing smelled. But if they offered doctored paperwork that made them look legitimate when they weren't, they were headed for the big house.

Did I mention that Slaid's column ran on Mondays and Fridays and that mine ran on Tuesdays and Thursdays? Well, it was Friday, and I sat down at my desk with a large Starbucks coffee, black, and a toasted bagel and butter, the soul-food breakfast of every New Yorker on the run. I flipped the pages of the paper and came to Slaid's column:

The Caribbean Film Fest
by Slaid Warren

City dwellers who want to escape from New York's snow and ice don't have to go far to bask in sunshine and enjoy snow-white beaches that are often empty. The U.S. Virgin Islands offer posh resorts where you can snorkel, scuba dive, eat fish caught fresh that morning and even…yes…negotiate sweet deals for Hollywood moviemakers who want a helping hand in using the resources of our city.

And the best part? Well, if you work for the Mayor's Office of Film, Theatre and Broadcasting, there's a chance that your winter escape will cost you nothing. Why? Because purportedly, you're there on business discussing things like getting tax deductions, acquiring appropriate studio space, finding cheap rental-car deals and hotel rooms, and closing the Brooklyn Bridge to rush-hour traffic...

The article went on to discuss Reilly and his film credits as well as his lavish style of entertaining. What Slaid didn't have was the damning documentation— at least not yet.

I gave the art department the receipts to photograph. Then I began to put together the story. All I needed was to call Reilly for comment before I finished. It was close to lunchtime and I lifted the receiver to phone a friend in the culture department to see if she wanted to have lunch with me. Just getting out of the office for an hour can help you decompress so that you come back to your work with a fresh perspective. I was so close to the story that I was beginning to feel as though I couldn't see it anymore.

It's always jarring to lift the phone to make a call and find someone already on the other end of it, as though they were eavesdropping on your life. I was a bit disoriented for a moment. The voice was familiar, but I couldn't place it.

"Hello, Jen."

I hesitated. "Who is this?"

"Jack...Jack Reilly."

"Jack," I said, fumbling. "How are you?" I felt my pulse start to race. Even though I needed to interview him before the story ran, I wanted to be calm, and prepared with my questions. He had caught me, unprepared.

"We need to talk," he said.

"Actually, I was going to call you to set something—"

"Marilyn called me," he said.

"I see."

"So now I think we should have a little tête-à-tête before your column runs."

"My day is terrible, but—"

"Don't run the column yet," he said.

"Forget it, Jack."

"You don't have the whole story," he said. I didn't say anything.

"Look, I know you have no reason to trust me, but I'll make it worth your while." That was a loaded last line. What was he implying? There was only one way that I could find out and I had only a few seconds to make a decision. Reilly was used to doing whatever it took to get people to do what he wanted. Why should I trust him? And why should I hold up a column that would decimate him? Still, my gut told me that if he wanted to see me that badly, there was more to the story, and it could be worth the risk to wait.

"Fine," I said. "Where?"

"The Waldorf," he said. "Seven o'clock."

Every columnist has to have a column or two called filler that they can dredge up when a planned piece is pulled or doesn't come together in time. I had done more research on misappropriation of funds for school libraries and much as I hated to use it, I called it up, filled in some holes and sent it in.

"More on libraries?" Marty said, shaking his head. "What the hell happened to your column on Reilly?"

"It's going to be an even better one. He wants to talk to me, apparently quite urgently."

"Where, in a hotel room?" I gave him a dirty look. I didn't dare tell him where we were meeting.

"He tried that, it didn't work," I said.

"Be careful," Marty said.

"I think he wants to come clean. His former assistant who's his ex-lover turned on him." Marty weighed that and shrugged.

"He wouldn't be the first guy to be done in because his brains are in his balls," he said. "But don't put things off too much longer."

I went home early to shower and change before meeting Reilly. Instead of the limp Banana Republic skirt I had thrown on that morning, I changed into a black Armani suit and heels. No, I wasn't trying to look good for him, I was trying to make myself feel more professional and more confident, even though I felt like such a lightweight when I was up against such a master manipulator. I was brushing my hair when I heard a key in the lock. That was odd. Chris said that he wouldn't be home for dinner. A moment later, the door opened and he looked as surprised as I did.

"Oh, you're home," he said before taking off his jacket.

"I was going to say the same thing to you. Is everything all right?" He looked at me for a minute before saying anything.

"Jen, I think we have to talk," he said, looking at the floor. I walked toward him and put my hairbrush down on the side of the couch before sitting down. I didn't need this right now, I had enough on my mind, but what choice did I have? He straddled the other arm of the couch and looked down and then up at me. I was getting that uneasy feeling that creeps up on you when someone is about to tell you something that you know you don't want to hear.

"I...I don't really know what to say," he said.

"Just say it," I said, shaking my head. I studied him as he had his head down and noticed what looked like the beginning of a goatee. I had never noticed the stubbly chin before.

"I'm seeing someone else," he blurted out. I sat there, immobile, staring back at him. He caught my eye for a minute to see how that registered, and then he looked off, but went on.

"You know ever since the campaign started, the whole group of us have been hanging out a lot." I nodded. "You went down to the Caribbean, and it just seemed like the house was empty, and so…well, you probably guessed that I was going out with Bridget."

So there it was, out in the open. Everything that I secretly dreaded was now confirmed. I was almost relieved to hear it.

"I guess that I better start looking for a new place," I said, getting up and starting to brush my hair again, now with greater intensity.

"Look, I don't want you to think you have to run out. You can stay here as long as you want…I feel really bad about it…we had good times…and I still love you, Jen, I care about you."

I looked at him and I didn't know whether to laugh or cry.

"You love me?" I said, tears in my eyes. "Well you have a hell of a way of showing it." Then, maybe because I was hanging around with Marilyn, and I felt some of the same venom that she did, I said, "Actually, I would have thought you would have gone for someone with more brains, but I obviously had you pegged wrong. You deserve her. I hope you have a great life together."

"Listen, things happen," he said, shaking his head as if my reaction was uncalled for. "It wasn't premeditated or anything. We were just together a lot, and she had broken up with the guy she was seeing, so she was sort of down…and you were so tied up with the job…" He let his voice drop off. I suppose

I should have been thankful *not* to hear him say she was just so fabulous looking that he couldn't resist. That was understood.

"And you weren't tied up with *your* job? Maybe I should have slept with someone to fill in the times when you were stuck at the office," I said. I didn't like the mudslinging that I was taking part in so enthusiastically, so instead, I just went into the bathroom and closed the door, trying to stifle my sobs by pressing my face up hard against a towel.

He knocked on the bathroom door and I sat down on the toilet seat, unable to open it.

"Listen," Chris said, "I just wanted to let you know that you can have the place to yourself for the next week or so." I opened the door an inch and looked at him.

"You're moving in with her?"

He nodded. "For now."

No wonder he had come home early. He wanted to pack. What would he have done if I wasn't there? Send me a note? A quick e-mail? Maybe, an e-card. "SURPRISE! OUR RELATIONSHIP IS OVER— START PACKING!" I looked at him and closed the door, kicking it behind me.

It was so awful that it was almost comical. I was so wound up that what came out of my throat was a wounded sound as though something had been thrown against me. The worst thing was the timing, just before the meeting with Reilly. I had to be strong, self-possessed, not crumbling like a distraught female whose boyfriend had walked out on her.

I thought back to that day on Buck Island when Reilly and I talked about his marriage and then my relationship. He said he had a hunch that the guy wasn't the one, and it had hit a nerve. Was it all so transparent?

I stayed in the bathroom until I heard Chris's key in the door. Did he pack the bag that I'd given him? Obviously I had sensed what was ahead. But no, that was ridiculous. I put cold compresses on my eyes, and used concealer to cover the awful pink on my eyelids and nose. Some brown eyeshadow, mascara, and then a few deep, calming breaths. Then I left the apartment, hoping that most of the evidence of my emotional unraveling was gone.

I got to Second Avenue where I tried unsuccessfully to hail a cab because I was wearing high heels. I thought about calling a car service, but I knew that it would take at least fifteen minutes until they showed up. At the same time, I kept thinking about Slaid's reaction to my upcoming column on libraries. What a big laugh he'd get. He called less these days, but he still called or did something sophomoric and annoying. In this case, he'd probably send a library card by messenger, or worse, a donation. He'd jump to the conclusion that since I didn't have his expertise, I wasn't able to get the goods on Reilly, so the paper pulled the column. While some other time I might have enjoyed the clever repartee, at this point, after the scene with Chris, my sense of humor had dried up.

It's one thing for a relationship to die a natural death—the attraction dwindles or one partner's life flourishes while the other's doesn't, what have you. But in our case, I felt like the one who'd created the road map for my own undoing, ending one of the most solid relationships that I had had in years. Why hadn't I had the foresight to see the implications of what I'd blurted out? But more important, did I really love Chris? Was I convinced that he was the one?

A former shrink of mine who was perpetually bombarded with dramlets about my various relationships always used to stop me from asking questions about guys' motivations. She'd turn to me and say, "But is he meeting your needs? What do *you* want?"

I'd been so consumed with being what I thought men like Chris wanted, I'd never asked myself that question. Was Chris meeting my needs? Did I want to marry him? Yes, no...I didn't know. I felt like one of those pathetic types who wrote to advice columnists asking, "How do you know if you're in love?"

Why didn't I know? Was it just that at this point I wasn't ready to make decisions about the future? I always assumed that if we stayed together long enough it would lead to something permanent. In the meantime, I was obsessed with thoughts of him and Bridget. Was it her looks alone that dazzled him, or her personality too? If it was just a physical attraction, would he get over it? Come back to me? It probably didn't hurt that the girl was a multimillionaire who lived in a fabulous apartment, not to mention a weekend place that was probably equally opulent. She'd have all kinds of fun toys to play with—designer bicycles, probably several cars, motorcycles. Still, Chris wasn't the material type. He liked earning money, but if he earned half of what he did, it wouldn't trouble him.

I thought back to Marilyn, and how she probably felt after her affair with Reilly lost steam. To make matters worse, he was married, so unless she was living in a dreamworld, she had to know that sooner or later, he would pull the plug on things.

Unable to find a cab, I walked downtown and then east for a few blocks until I was in front of New York University Hospital. Cabs were always pulling up and I waited until one stopped. It took a few moments for the door to open. I waited, and then saw the woman inside pay the driver and then ease her way out, as if the movement was agonizingly painful. She was pale, weak, no more than forty, with a pretty but unsmiling face. Her head was wrapped in a red bandanna scarf. I reached out my hand to help support her.

"Oh, that's okay," she said, finally pulling herself up. She caught her breath and then started to make her way toward the door. No, it's not okay, I wanted to say. She didn't deserve to be wearing that scarf, or thinking about sickness and loss instead of life and joy and all the trivial concerns that the healthy fill their days with. I glanced at the way her slacks hung loose against her slight frame as she walked, taking small steps through the hospital door. Would she come out again? Would she get a second chance? I'd been spared problems like hers. I was free to live life and think about my future. I had had a good year with Chris and life would go on. I'd meet other men, have other relationships. I was thirty-six years old and I hoped to have years and years of good life before me. I turned to walk the other way, remembering her downcast eyes.

Chapter Sixteen

I arrived at the Waldorf calmer, and cut through the bustling lobby, making my way to the dark mahogany bar at the Bull and Bear Steakhouse. The service would be fast, the drinks strong. It was the perfect place to talk about the unraveling of someone's life.

Reilly was seated at the bar with his hand around a glass of scotch. He swiveled around as I walked up to him and sat on the bar stool next to him.

"Thanks for coming," he said. He looked at me with a small smile on his face. No matter what he was thinking, Reilly always looked as if admiring a woman was the first thing on his mind. I turned away momentarily, breaking eye contact.

"What are you drinking?" he asked as the bartender approached.

"White wine," I said, even though a dry martini seemed more appropriate.

"I got a table," he said after my drink arrived. The waiter carried our glasses over and we sat down at a round table covered with a starched white cloth. What I really wanted was to just sit back and enjoy what was sure to be a fabulous steak dinner. I wanted to finish the glass of wine and then order another and forget about the story, and about Chris and the fact that I'd have to move out of our apartment. All I wanted was to laugh, make small talk and be distracted and pretend that he was someone else, someone with a private jet who could fly me down to a posh resort for a weekend so that I could assume the role of society princess instead of hardworking, underpaid journalist. But instead, the meal would be wasted on me. Knowing that I was about to write a column that was sure to indict him took the edge off my appetite.

"You're still tan," Reilly said.

"I think it's more of a windburn from the storm," I said, smiling briefly. The waiter handed us menus, but neither of us looked at them. "Rib eye, rare, with fries," he said. I ordered the same.

"So what is it?" I asked, studying his face, aware of a small area of his chin where he had nicked himself while shaving.

"You met Marilyn," he said.

I nodded.

"What did you think of her?"

"Smart, tough. I wouldn't want her as my enemy." He smiled.

"I never intended to hurt her. We had an intimate relationship, but things change and you grow apart. At that point it makes no sense to continue working together on a day-to-day basis. She didn't see it that way."

"Did you expect her to just smile benignly and walk away?"

"I thought she was tougher than she is," Jack said. "I thought she could handle a relationship with a married man. I never made any pretenses, but clearly I was wrong, and now I'm paying the price."

"What did she tell you about our meeting?" I asked, not showing my hand.

"You did your job well," he said. "I know what you have. She kept copies of everything."

"I wondered how you were able to convince Alex and the gang to be your guests," I said. "She explained that to me."

"Despite what you may think about it, I've known these people for a long time. We had business to discuss. I'm part owner of the hotel so it didn't cost me anything, and it really wasn't a big deal to invite them to come down for a few days to go over details. It's winter, who doesn't want to get away?"

I nodded, and he went on.

"Anyway, we wanted to work in the city, not give

the business to the Canadians," he said. "It didn't hurt the country or the city, just the opposite. I single-handedly brought in tens of millions of dollars." Hmm, I thought to say, maybe they should have a ticker-tape parade for you.

It always amazes me how people can explain away things that they have done wrong and, in fact, knew were wrong at the time. It is as though the laws simply didn't apply to them, or were just plain irrelevant. He must have gathered my cynicism from the expression on my face.

"I've done things wrong over the past five years," Jack said. "I don't deny that. But now that I've made all the money that I could possibly want, it doesn't matter. Everything's falling apart," he said, "and you know what? I don't give a goddamn anymore."

I looked at him strangely. I'd never met anyone like Jack Reilly. He was a real curiosity to me. The Hollywood honcho from a rarefied world who made his own rules. I sat there waiting for him to go on. Part of me wanted to pull out the notebook that I had in my purse, or click on the tape recorder, but I knew he wouldn't talk as freely. Clearly, everything was on the record, but he wouldn't be as relaxed if I were scribbling away.

"You might not believe this," Jack said, "but when you and I were sitting together on the beach talking about people getting married on the boat, it struck me that despite all the success I've had on a business level and all my relationships with women, I wasn't happy with my life, or the way that I was living it. I really did want to stay and get away from everything." He looked at me intently.

I looked back at him, trying to decide how much of what he was saying was truthful, and how much was designed to seduce me to the point of being kind to him—in print. If he was acting, he was doing a bang-up job.

"Anyway," he went on, "I've decided that I'm getting out of the business. I've given the city notice that someone else is taking my place as the head of production, and over the course of the next few months, I'll be meeting with my lawyers to close the company."

To say that I was shocked was an understatement. And because deep down my gut instincts are always to believe that someone is telling the truth, despite the kind of stories that fill my newspaper indicating that the opposite is usually the case, part of me wanted to say that it was okay, that I was killing the column and all the damning evidence that I had against him. I waited for him to go on, but he just sat there, staring at me. He reached over to put his hand over mine.

"You're full of surprises," I said, pulling my hand back. "I wish it were otherwise, Jack, but you know that I can't hold back what I have."

"I didn't expect you to," he said. "But now you

know there's more to the story, and I figured that I'd give it to you instead of having Slaid Warren report it with his particular slant."

"He's a pretty good reporter," I said, not knowing why I felt that I had to defend Slaid.

"He said the same thing about you." That surprised me. Maybe it was just his way of showing Jack that he was an all right guy.

"That's a switch."

"What does it take to break through that protective bubble around you?" Reilly said. I couldn't help feeling his presence closing in on me, like air that was imperceptibly filling with poison gas. I looked back at him in his five-thousand-dollar black silk Brioni suit with the cool yellow silk necktie and wondered what he liked more, the women or the challenge.

The food came and we sat there for a few minutes without talking as we ate. Finally, I turned to him.

"There's no protective bubble," I said. "I just try to keep my professional life separated from my personal life."

"I tried that too," Reilly said. "So much for my resolve." I started to laugh, and so did he.

"So what are you going to do now?" I asked, changing the direction we were going in.

"Meet with my lawyers and try to straighten things out," he said, as if he assumed that he could unwrite history if he had the right legal defense. Of course, he was partially right. He paused and then added, "And my wife and I are filing for divorce." I looked up at him, surprised. It was none of my business, but I asked anyway.

"Was that her idea or yours?"

"Mutual."

"She knew about your dalliances," I said, unable to help myself. "Why did she stay with you?" He looked at me as if the answer was obvious.

"Love."

"So where is your new life going to take you?"

"I'm going to buy a place in the Caribbean and live down there for a while. I'll buy a boat and..." He shrugged. "We'll see."

It struck me that our encounter might have been responsible for changing the course of his life. I wondered whether he wanted to thank me or murder me.

"I hope you can start over when all of this is behind you."

"I have to try," he said. At that moment, the waiter came over to clear our table and handed us both dessert menus.

"Devil's food cake?" Reilly asked with a wink.

I shook my head, sliding my chair back. "I have to get back."

He motioned for the check. I was going to get up and leave him at the table paying the bill—then thought better of it. After being in this business for a while, I've learned that the moment you think the interview is over and put away your notebook, you sometimes get your best material. I waited while he signed the check and then we walked out together toward the street.

"I'll get you a cab."

I'm fine," I said, starting to flag down a cab as it pulled up to the front door. He opened the door for me and I stood there for a moment. "Which way are you going? Can I drop you off?"

"I've got a suite upstairs," he said. He turned to me. "I've brought millions of dollars into New York. No one was hurt. Isn't that more important than pointing a finger at a few people?"

"You can't operate outside the law, Jack."

He shook his head in frustration. "I'm sorry we didn't meet under other circumstances. We would have enjoyed each other."

I nodded and my cab sped off. After a few minutes, it occurred to me that I hadn't asked him whether he was pulling out of his investment in the Caribbean hotel as well. I dialed the hotel and asked for Jack Reilly. A moment passed, and then I heard the phone ringing. On the third ring, a woman answered. I hung up without saying anything. The voice struck me as familiar, but I couldn't place it. Just as the cab reached the front door of my building, I realized who it was.

When I walked through the door of Chris's apartment now it seemed as though I were returning to someone else's place, and an earlier chapter in my life. I felt like a stranger to the man I had been sleeping with. So what did I do? I started to look through Chris's drawers. What was I hoping to accomplish? Evidence, I guess. I was curious to know where he had been taking her, how serious it was, what would happen between them—everything, really. Methodically, I went through his underwear drawer, his desk drawers, even his appointment book, like a thief combing for any nugget of value.

What I found: not a lot. There were receipts for dinners for the week when I was away, but they certainly didn't indicate that he had been taking her to four-star restaurants or had been shopping in fancy Madison Avenue boutiques. Of course. Why would they go out to dinner in top restaurants when they could frolic in her giant hot tub and screw on her white silk lounges overlooking Central Park. As far as gifts, no, Chris didn't shower women with luxurious trinkets, but anyway, what could she possibly need?

Most models I knew dressed down when they weren't working, as if they made a point of trying to look as plain as a gorgeous girl could look which, of course, had the opposite effect, accentuating their perfection. Still, I felt as though I wanted to know the enemy and I kept on checking. After desk drawers, bureau drawers and the basket of odds and ends near the phone didn't reveal much, I thought of one more place to investigate: Chris's laptop.

Did I dare go through his e-mails? That really smacked of sleaziness and distrust. It was base and un-ethical, like going through someone's diary. Once the thought took possession of me, however, I couldn't get rid of it. What the hell, the relationship was in the gutter. He had cheated on *me,* why should I take the high road? As far as unethical, he'd raised the bar.

I sat down and opened his Outlook Express e-mail program, going through various files, but most of them were filled with e-mails about passwords and user IDs and the occasional business transaction or notice of upcoming meetings. Then I went to Sent Mail. That way I could read the e-mails that he'd sent her or at least how he'd replied to hers. I went through a bunch of back-and-forths with the office, and then came to an ID—Bridgetcvrgrl. Obviously when Bridget wasn't posing in front of a camera, she enjoyed sending out e-mails. There must have been a hundred. I scanned through some of them.

Sounds cool, I'll call you later—was his response to:

Hey Chris, finish at 4. Wanna order Pizza and try the Jacuzzi? Need to have fun, this day is A DISASTER!

Can't wait. Thanks Bridge came after:

My masseuse is coming over at 7. She's great. (And so am I!) Want a massage?
I'll pick up some sushi. Call me!

Bridge—stuck at the office. The campaign is swallowing up my life. Want to come up here and keep me company? Otherwise I'll meet you at your place. Keep the bed warm. Chris

And from Bridgetcvrgrl: I'll be waiting in bed. Totally YOURS, B

And finally the one from her inviting him up to her country place. He replied: So hot to see you, I'm ready to run outta this place now. C After she wrote:

Come with me to Connecticut. We can sleep late and go sledding. It'll be fun to just get away together, don't you think? Kisses and more, B

So hot to see her? And keep the bed warm? I could do that. I wanted to get a can of gasoline and light a match under his bed. I resisted the temptation to slam the screen. My other temptation was to turn off his antivirus program so that he'd come back to a laptop full of viruses. Was there a Web site where you could pick up viruses to send them to others—justdeserts.com?

I packed enough clothes for a couple of days. If it was okay with Ellen, I'd go to her apartment. If not, I'd go to a hotel. I liked small boutique hotels, so I could pretend that I was just getting away for a few days. Even though Chris probably wouldn't be coming back to sleep, I hated the idea of spending another night in the bed that we'd shared. I called Ellen.

"My guest room's ready," she said. "It's all yours." I already had her keys.

When my tote bag was packed, I grabbed my laptop and locked the door behind me.

I entered Ellen's apartment on East Seventy-second Street and felt as though I was beginning a new life. How long would it be until I had a place of my own? This was like going back in time. No doubt I'd end up with a studio apartment. With rents and co-op prices what they were, one room would probably be all that I could afford. Ellen was already asleep, so I locked the door and went into the guest room. It was cozy, inviting, painted forest green. Against the wall was a queen-size brass bed covered with a pale yellow and white Amish quilt. A stack of folded white towels were at the foot of the bed. The walls were lined with bookshelves. I walked around the room looking at the pictures that she had on some of the shelves. There was a new one that I hadn't seen in a small Adirondack-style wooden frame. It was a picture of Ellen and Moose standing on the edge of a mountain in their snowshoes. They both looked red cheeked and healthy, wearing thick jackets and hats. They had big smiles on their faces as though they welcomed having their picture taken and that moment in time recorded.

Did I have pictures of me and Chris? Somewhere. I wanted to study them now to see if we looked that happy together. We hadn't traveled much together since one of us was always tied up when the other was free. And if we did take pictures, what would they tell me? Would I be able to divine how well we had related to each other? Would his expression tell me how close he'd felt to me? There were psychics who could look at current pictures of people and intuit enough information to tell you what was going on in their lives. Would I be able to look into Chris's eyes and know what was ahead for him, or for us?

I washed up and undressed, slipping between the fresh white sheets. I was just a guest in Ellen's house, but I felt as though life had arbitrarily relocated me to an unfamiliar world. I was single again, unattached, but this time, instead of feeling free and open to new relationships, I felt as though life had deserted me. With more and more time passing, my options were running out. Breakups were harder when you were older, and whether it was justified or not, I began to feel as though some personal failure of mine was behind the fact that I couldn't link up with someone who was right for me, while just about every other woman, good-looking or not, smart or not, successful or not, managed to find someone to spend her life with.

"Every pot has its cover," my grandmother used to say. Well, this pot was still uncovered, exposed and ready to boil over.

Ellen would already be gone when I got up in the morning. She was energetic, committed, a real dynamo when it came to getting things done. Maybe she was the perfect match for Moose. I pulled the covers up around me. Instead of relationships, I fell asleep thinking about Reilly and the column. I didn't look forward to writing it. It was never fun to do pieces that were basically character assassinations. Still, it would be a bombshell. It would blow Slaid out of the water.

The next morning, after stopping for coffee, I made my way into the office, arriving earlier than usual. It was quiet, almost deserted. Good, I wasn't in the mood to make small talk with my colleagues or overhear their phone conversations as I was writing. There was no privacy in the office. No one had offices, they had cubicles, and inevitably voices rose above the overall din. If someone's kids didn't get into a school, or if someone had to refinance their mortgage, you not only heard about it, you heard it being discussed and then analyzed as the recipient talked to others and chewed it over. I remember writing one column while hearing a blow-by-blow of the birth process right down to "nine centimeters dilated," and then the "crowning."

I sat down at my computer and pressed the power button. I was about to go right to work, but before I did, I opened the *Trib* to glance at what Slaid had done. I started reading and immediately put my coffee cup down and pushed my chair away from the computer. His column started out about the benefits of taking up residence in St. Croix, and then zeroed in on Reilly.

Warm weather, sunlit skies and pristine beaches are just one reason to buy an ice cream-colored home in the U.S. Virgin Islands. Another one is to dodge the need to share your hard-earned money with Uncle Sam.

It went on to discuss how growing numbers of wealthy Americans had taken up residence in the Virgin Islands over the past few years because an economic development program there confers big tax benefits. More detail on the incentive followed and then this:

Among the bigwigs to buy property in St. Croix is Jack Reilly, president and CEO of Reilly Films. His name may mean nothing to you unless you've been following the inside-baseball stuff of making movies. Ask our mayor about Reilly, or better yet, the mayor's staff in his film office. They've spent time with Reilly on the most beautiful beaches in the world, putting

their heads together about things like housing movie production crews and opening the Statue of Liberty for night filming, all the while sharing beach-barbecue dinners and drinking piña coladas while watching orange sunsets.

Slaid had discovered that Reilly purchased a two-million-dollar estate a year before and had established residency, raising questions, first, about whether the move—like so many others—was legitimate. Then he'd linked him to the financing of upcoming films, asking how logistically it would be possible to run his operation from his beachside villa.

I threw the paper down. I felt like calling Slaid to thank him for getting my adrenaline level soaring. Not only was I going to write my column, I was already sharpening my sword. Here I was feeling sorry for the bastard, only to discover that Reilly had already bought his Caribbean villa, not really as a getaway, but to avoid paying taxes. My fingers hit the keys, and for the next two hours, I wrote as though my hands were on fire. I laid out every detail of my trip, including the papers to show who had visited the resort, when, and how the bills were doctored to look as though the film office employees had paid. I tried to get comments from the three film department employees, only to get two mumbled "no comments," and one denial of any wrongdoing, "'I was there on business for the city,' that's all I'm going to say."

At nine-thirty, I called Reilly in his New York office.

"He's tied up in a meeting," his secretary said.

"Tell him to untie himself," I said. "I need to talk to him." I held for what seemed like an eternity. Finally he picked up the phone.

"Jen—"

"Did you establish residency in St. Croix?" I asked, skipping the usual pleasantries.

"I've had that house for a couple of years," he said, exhaling for effect. "I intended to live there, but I've been pulled in ten different directions."

"Was that a yes or a no, Jack?"

"It isn't the way Warren painted it. Listen, that was exactly what I was talking about and why I gave you the story," he said, as if it was wearying for him to go over something he had already gone over. "He wanted to make headlines and he got carried away with himself."

I paused for a minute. "You know what, Jack," I said, tapping the edge of a pen against the edge of the table like a drummer. "I think you're bullshitting me."

"You guys want things reduced to sound bites, Jen. Life isn't like that."

"Is that what you tell the feds when they come knocking on your door?"

"Listen, let's talk about this over dinner."

"I don't think so," I said, and hung up.

★ ★ ★

When my column came out the following day with the headline Living in Dreamland, it triggered more calls and e-mails than anything I had ever written.

"Terrific job," Marty said—his most effusive praise. Colleagues who usually walked past me in the corridor offering nothing more than a nod offered high fives, whistles and extravagant praise, one of them making knife-sharpening motions. My love life might be in tatters, but my career seemed to be at an all-time high.

I was heading away from my desk to go to lunch when the phone rang. I hesitated, and then went back to pick it up.

"Nice piece of work."

"Now I'm worried," I said.

"Why?" Slaid asked.

"Because you're never one to praise me," I said.

"I told you he was a sleaze, but you don't know the half of it."

I knew what I had missed would enter into the conversation. It was only a matter of time. "So tell me what I left out," I said.

"I will," he said, "before too long, along with our other nine hundred thousand readers."

"Thanks for the call," I said dryly. Then, feeling more vulnerable than usual, and annoyed by his perpetually cutting remarks, at a time when everyone else was praising me, I decided to tell him how I felt.

"Slaid," I said, "why don't we just stop this infantile exchange of calls. You want to jerk off, do it without me on the other end." I hung up before he could answer.

Chapter Seventeen

With everything going on, a week had gone by and I had forgotten to tell Ellen about Kelly Cartwright. She rarely took time during the day, but I told her that she'd be interested in what I'd found. We agreed to meet at a small seafood restaurant in midtown. I got there first and sat sipping a San Pellegrino while trying to catch up with the other papers that I inevitably toted around to read in between appointments.

"So what's up?" Ellen said breathlessly, sliding into the seat facing mine. She was wearing a fabulous black-and-white Chanel suit. Only I knew that she'd bought it at a resale store. Instead of looking tired and strained, she had a glow.

"I know it has to do with Moose," she said.

"You're not going to believe this," I said. She sat

there, wide-eyed, waiting. I was about to start, when the waiter came by to take our order.

"Salmon for both of us," I said, knowing without asking what she'd have. "Cooked through." She nodded. We inevitably ordered the same thing. Salmon, shrimp, maybe snapper. Never beef. Never pork. And rarely the all-vegetarian entrée. There was a limit to the sacrifices we made for good health.

"So here goes," I said when the waiter turned away. "Guess who was having an affair with that nonentity Kelly Cartwright?"

"Tell me."

"Jack Reilly."

"What?" She shook her head in disbelief.

"That was what I read about him," she said, as if she suddenly remembered. "'Page Six,' of course," she said, slamming her hand on the table. "It was one of those sketchy items, but there was no doubt."

"She got the role in *Living on the Edge* because of Reilly," I said. "And after the movie was over she enjoyed being away from the Hollywood scene so much that she decided to stay for a while." Although no one ever confirmed that Moose was the guy she was living with, we were convinced that it was him.

"So why did she end the relationship with Moose?" Ellen asked.

"Don't hold me to this," I said, "but according to my sources in culture, she started seeing Jack romantically just before the filming. He expected her to leave when the movie wrapped and he wasn't too happy about her taking time off and secluding herself. But she stayed for a month or so, and at that point, to lure her back to Hollywood he told her that he wanted to talk to her about a role in a chick-lit film that had a major star cancel out at the last minute. He flew her to Hawaii and they spent the weekend together."

"Quel sleaze," Ellen said.

I nodded. "His fascination with her lasted for a few weeks, and then he moved on to a Catherine Zeta-Jones look-alike."

"Well, what we don't know for sure is that she was the one who lived with Moose," Ellen said. "Did anyone see them together?" I opened my purse and took out a picture of the two of them that ran in the local paper that the research department found for me. I slid it across the table to Ellen.

She glanced down. "Case closed."

After the salmon, and lemon sorbet, we talked about work and then Chris.

"I haven't been this down since my apartment was robbed," I said, remembering when a former handyman in my building had let himself into several apartments and left the job, never to be found, with our cash and jewelry.

"What you do to get yourself out of that kind of funk is help someone else," Ellen said. She took a deep breath.

"Uh-oh," I said. "Are you asking me to give up a kidney?"

She shook her head. "Here's my idea. I've been working on a project to help the homeless, particularly schoolkids. But it's such a miserable situation and as usual I don't feel as though I'm doing enough just by helping a few families, so I've been trying to come up with other things that I can do."

I looked at Ellen. She should have become an aid worker or a legal-aid lawyer, not a TV reporter. She really was the kind of person who would give you half of her last bite of food, if not all of it. I looked back at her, wishing I could measure up.

"Then it occurred to me to use my network connections to host a fund-raiser," she said. "If you're part of it, we can bring together TV and news types, not to mention all the celebrities that we have access to so that we can raise money to make a real difference."

I had given money to the United Way, I'd walked to raise money for AIDS and breast cancer research, but I had never done anything more ambitious. There was certainly no political reason why I couldn't participate, and if Ellen was part of it... Also, working on the benefit was a worthwhile way to take up my nights and weekends so that I wouldn't have spare time to lie around sulking and feeling sorry for myself. I couldn't remember the last time that I had done anything meaningful to help others.

"Great idea," I said. "It can be our Valentine's Day present to the city."

For the next two weeks, we spent all our free time looking for locations, restaurants to give us donations, and large-ticket donors. It would be a black-tie event and ultimately we decided to do it outdoors, in a white tent that we would erect outside a restaurant. We planned the event for a few days before Valentine's Day, so the theme was a natural: Have a Heart.

There are times when New York shows its largesse, and its warm, compassionate spirit—often buried below self-protective layers—rises to the surface. This was one of them. I collected pledges of catered food from prominent restaurants and stores. We collected raffle prizes ranging from Knicks tickets, luggage and jewelry, to donated weekends at Hamptons beach houses.

"Are you actually going to sit down and do some work?" Marty asked when he heard me one afternoon later that week in the corridor talking to some other reporters about the event.

"What gives, Marty? You're grumpier than usual."

"I got a call from Jack Reilly's lawyer. They're thinking of suing us for defamation of character."

"On what basis?"

"He'll come up with something." Marty said flatly.

"If he only knew what we *didn't* use," I said, thinking of all the tidbits about Reilly's love life that would have been perfect for the gossip column, including the voice on the phone at the Waldorf who I realized was a barely legal actress who was in one of his upcoming films. Some of his other flames, if there was truth to the rumors, were celebrating their sweet sixteens.

Marty shrugged. "I think he was just trying to intimidate us, or at the least, find out if we're working on a follow-up."

"I could spend my whole career investigating Reilly. But to what end? Everyone knows his number now, and I doubt whether he'll be as blatant anymore, assuming that he stays in the business, which he says he isn't."

"Let's wait for the indictments to come in. That will be our peg for starting the ball rolling again."

Things were moving along pretty smoothly, and for once I felt as though I was doing something worthwhile. It might have been my upbeat mood, but I started thinking about Chris again. This time I didn't feel angry, just curious. I missed him, I did. I didn't realize how much I welcomed coming home to him at the end of the day and the way we shared stories of what went on. I was still camping out at Ellen's, and it was no fun being in someone else's empty apartment.

I tried to imagine his new life with Bridget. There

must have been lots of parties and openings to attend. Models were always invited to improve the
scenery. I thought of the expression *arm candy*. Idi-
otic, offensive; still, in this case, it seemed to fit. Was
she his arm candy? Did it up his status at the agency
to be dating her? Guys were probably all over her,
how did that sit with him?

I was sure his name would start appearing in
gossip columns as the mystery man she had alluded
to on TV. I also wondered how the client would
like that. Would it help sales of Model Thin?
Maybe she wasn't hypoglycemic and crabby. Or
defensive about her career. Maybe she was not only
beautiful, but easy to live with. Clearly, cooking
and cleaning weren't issues. She could afford lots
of help, end of story. Amid it all, I wondered if
sometimes he still thought of me. Did he miss me
at all and think of the life that we had together?
And if he did, would he have the nerve to pick up
the phone?

For the rest of the day, I was consumed with the
idea of calling him just to hear his voice and find
out how he was. Despite my compulsiveness, I decided to hold off and think about it before I did
anything.

What did I hope to accomplish by phone? Did
I expect him to say it was all a big mistake? I
thought back to how our relationship started. I
called him. He said that he was going to call me

but he never did. After going out to lunch and mulling over all the possible scenarios, I decided it was infantile to rehearse it. So the moment I got back to my desk, I lifted the phone—so much for my reserve.

So what, the little voice in my head kept saying. Just because we broke up didn't mean that we had to stop speaking. We had a lot of shared history to- gether—why did we have to become total strangers. The phone rang and on the second ring he answered.

"Hi," I said, wondering if I now needed to iden- tify myself. No, that was ridiculous. He'd moved on to another woman, but he didn't have amnesia.

"Hey, Jen," he said, not sounding particularly sur- prised, but not particularly thrilled either. "How're you doing?"

"I'm okay," I said, as if I was trying to convince myself that I was. "How about you?"

"Working a lot," he said. There was an awkward silence.

"Maybe you need a break."

"Yeah, actually, I was going to call you. Are you still staying at my place?"

"No," I said. "Why?" I was actually thinking about moving back in though. I'd decided that it wasn't fair to keep imposing on Ellen.

"I'm going out of town for a while."

"Oh, where?"

He paused, as if deciding whether to tell me. But Chris was never one to play games.

"Paris and Rome."

"Nice," I said. "With Bridget?"

"Yeah, she has to go on a fashion thingie, and she wants me to come along."

"How long are you staying?"

"Two weeks. I just wanted to let you know so that you could have the apartment to yourself if you need it, or wanted to stay." He sounded awkward, uncomfortable. Obviously he must have realized how hard it was for me to find another place. New Yorkers didn't leave their apartments until they died or won the lottery. It was that hard, and expensive, to find a place.

But what really stuck in my craw at that moment was thinking about all the times that I wanted to go away and how I could never get him to take more than a long weekend. We drove up to the Cape once. Big deal. But now, suddenly, he had arranged to go away for two weeks, and it wasn't even summer. Where would they stay, the George V? The Ritz? Her agency was probably putting them up in grand style. Not only was the ditz going to Europe where I was dying to go with my boyfriend, she was staying in hotels that I couldn't afford, and probably modeling designer clothes that would then be thrown her way as a *petit cadeau*. It always made me laugh how models and Hollywood stars, the only ones who could afford designer clothes and jewels, got them from the designers as gifts.

"Nice," I said, not bothering to disguise the coldness in my voice. "I hope you have a blast."

"Let's try to be friends, at least. I don't want to feel alienated from you."

No, we should embrace each other, take joy in all the good times we had. Take joy in the new directions that life is taking us. Life was short, why be bitter? Yeah, right.

Unfortunately, Chris didn't get involved with a woman blessed with a warm, benevolent spirit. I was bitter, and I felt more alone than ever. You screwed me over, I wanted to say, but I didn't.

"I gotta go," I said quickly. I hung up and took the paperweight with the name of his advertising agency on it and threw it into the bottom of the garbage pail along with a picture of him that I had snapped when he was vegging out in front of the TV one day.

With him on his way to the most romantic cities in the world, I moved back into the apartment. I wanted to have my own things around me. But everywhere I turned, I saw reminders of Chris—from his beer in the refrigerator to his old hairbrush in the bathroom and his posters on the wall.

Would he move in with her permanently and give up the apartment or just stay there occasionally, once I was gone? He probably didn't even think that far ahead. I was the practical one, trying to decide where to go, what to take. How did you divide a couch? The photograph of the empty highway out in West Texas that we both loved that was up in the kitchen? I leaned over and smelled his pillow. It held his scent. It registered with me viscerally by now on some deep biological level like my mother's Joy perfume, or the smell of the soup that my grandmother made every time I visited.

I picked up the *Times* real estate section and started going through the ads, circling the appropriate ones, aghast, as usual, at the prices. There weren't many options. I wanted to stay in Manhattan—so I could live and work in the same zip code. That meant that I'd probably end up in a studio apartment because the rentals on the one and two bedrooms were prohibitive. That was okay. A studio apartment could be cozy, womblike. Nothing got lost, there was no place for it to go.

After circling the ads that I wanted to call on, I made a list of corporations that I could hit up for donations to our party. I'd already called the publisher of my paper, next I'd try the *Trib,* Slaid's paper.

We hadn't talked since my nasty outburst, although he did send one e-mail with the subject line that read, "Addendum to hang-up." I deleted the message without opening it. He deserved it, he'd acted infantile, and since he'd never as much as throw me a crumb, what was the point of the clever repartee? Still, I suppose that I had regrets. It wasn't necessary to be testy and hostile. I could have just said that I preferred not to converse with the competition. Did the drama critic from the *Times* talk to the drama critic from the *Post?* Did *The New Yorker* talk to *New York Magazine* about its coverage? Of course not. So why did we have to engage in such ridiculous exchanges?

But now, I was concerning myself with something real, and I was sure that the *Trib* would want to be part of it. We were all on the side of helping kids. So when the assistant to the publisher told me that they wouldn't be contributing to my effort, needless to say, I was surprised.

"Oh, I'm disappointed," I said.

"Well, Ms. George," the publisher's assistant said, "it's not that we don't support your effort, it's just that this year, the *Trib* has decided to host a fund-raiser of its own."

"Oh," I said, surprised.

"Yes," she said. "We were motivated by all the stories on TV and in the papers about the homeless, so we're holding a fund-raiser just before Valentine's Day too."

I didn't say anything for a minute.

"Really? Who's heading up the effort," I said. "Maybe we can join forces."

"Well, that would be up to the publisher," she said.

"Can I talk with him?"

"He's out of town, Ms. George. But you can talk to the committee chair."

"Fine," I said. "What's her name?"

"Actually, it's a him," she said. "Slaid Warren."

Chapter Eighteen

There's nothing that does a better job at chipping away at your sense of self than an apartment search. No matter your budget, it's a paltry sum in the eyes of a real estate agent. They gloat over the fact that you're competing with people who are better off, urging you to grab that downstairs apartment, never mind that it's dark and dank.

After giving up on finding a decent rental, I looked into buying a co-op. Yes, I'd have to plunk down a chunk of money, but assuming I could get it together, I was planning for my future and real estate was always a sound investment. I started looking on Manhattan's Upper East Side, but when I found out that prices in doorman buildings were really out of my reach, I moved on to the West Side, and finally down to the Village.

I kept looking and eventually came upon a studio in a building on University Place in the Village. It was a prewar building with some small studio apartments that had a view of Washington Square Park just across the street. After putting down a binder, about ten percent of the purchase price, I began to put together all my financial information, not to mention those ridiculous letters of recommendation that would then be scrutinized by the co-op board who would then rule on my acceptability as a neighbor.

"Just write it yourself and I'll sign it," Marty said when I asked him to write a letter testifying to my upstanding character. I had also asked Ellen and a federal judge who had become a tennis partner to write letters on my behalf, and those went a long way to compensate for my lack of a million-dollar salary. Within a week, I had collected all the financial documents that I needed and then turned my thoughts back to the fundraiser. I didn't relish the thought of contacting Slaid, but I knew that I had to. He was trying to one-up me again, and I was determined to confront him. But first, I decided to use my column—writing a story in two parts—as a forum for laying out the problem and then soliciting donations. I usually don't do things like that, but in this case, I made an exception, and fortunately my editor didn't object.

What Men Want

No Place Called Home

Eight-year-old Laverne Jones doesn't go to bed the same time each night the way other boys his age do. And he doesn't sit down at the dinner table at six or seven or even eight the way other boys do.

Why?

Because he doesn't have a bed of his own, a place to have breakfast or dinner. In fact, he doesn't even have a place called home. Laverne and his mother, Laura, are two of the many thousands of New Yorkers who were evicted from their apartments because they couldn't pay the rent. So now, they are shuttled from one part of the city to the other where City Services assigns them to spend the night. School, when he can get there, is a poor elementary school in the Bronx that doesn't have enough chairs for all the students or even rooms to put them.

When it was Christmastime, Laverne Jones didn't find any gifts under the Christmas tree, because when you're homeless you don't have a tree or a place to put one if you did. Christmas is a holiday that you celebrate in your head, because there's no money for presents and not even for a Christmas dinner. On Christmas Day, Laverne and his mother went to McDonald's and had a hamburger and fries. Then they went back to the city office to wait around until they were told where they could spend the night.

And then my pitch:

Put Your Money Where Your Heart Is

Instead of buying your loved one Belgian chocolate for Valentine's Day, French champagne or long-stemmed roses, you can show your heart's in the right place by giving to kids who aren't showered with love and affection. At eight o'clock on Saturday evening, I'm proud to announce that I'm joining forces with TV reporter Ellen Gaines to host a fund-raiser to help kids who through no fault of their own don't have a place called home.

I usually don't use this space to advertise for needy causes, but the number of kids without homes is growing every year, and none of us can afford to look away. Imagine your life without a regular bed to sleep in. Without a refrigerator to hold eggs and bread. Without a place to shower. Imagine not knowing where you were going after school—assuming you even went to school. Imagine sleeping on the subway or bus because you were exhausted and didn't have a bed of your own.

About 17,000 kids in New York don't have to imagine what it would be like—they know….

The column brought an outpouring of support, not only from colleagues, but also from readers who were happy to find someone in the media using her clout for the public good.

"We're getting tremendous interest," Ellen said a day later. She did her part by making a quick announcement of the benefit on the morning news show, even though she was never on camera at that hour.

Interesting that Slaid didn't call. But then I opened the paper and saw how he'd filled his space.

Open Your Heart and Open Your Home

Instead of thinking of buying gifts for a loved one this Valentine's Day, how about showing your love of New York by hosting a small dinner party devoted to raising money for people who don't have homes of their own? This is a call to New Yorkers to gather around their dinner tables the weekend before Valentine's Day. You don't have to live on Park Avenue to take part. You don't have to have a real dining room at all. And your party doesn't have to be large. It doesn't have to be elaborate. Just a party of six, eight, ten people or twelve, depending on the size of your apartment or house. Instead of having your guests bring wine or dessert, ask them to make a donation to help the homeless…it's as simple as that.

I hated to admit it, but his approach was brilliant. Instead of feeling intimated about coming to a black-tie event, or writing a check that was sizable enough, he suggested a more modest effort that could have a far wider reach and involve more people than we could ever hope to bring in. Smart. Destined to succeed. But I resented his imitating our project, and taking some of the wattage out of our effort by staging his at the same time.

But I'd be big about it. I wouldn't call him or denigrate his effort. We were both working for the good of people who had a lot less than we did. He'd oversee his network of parties and I'd host the black-tie fund-raiser with Ellen. A lot of money was needed, and one plan wouldn't bring it all in.

If Chris were in town, I would have called his agency to help with advertising. But he wasn't, and I called someone at Omnicom, the biggest ad agency I knew. I was beginning to accept that he was gone and it was over. I thought of him in Paris, watching Bridget pose for covers of French and Italian *Vogue*. I enjoyed imagining him squirming in his seat as she spent hours having her makeup done and her clothes fitted and accessorized before she got to the point of sitting in front of the camera. And then once she did, I imagined him sitting by idly as the photographer moved her this way and that until he got the right picture. It would torture him.

I remembered the one and only time that he came with me to keep me company while I had a manicure. He sat there, uncomfortable, as if he had come from outer space and didn't understand what he was seeing. Finally, he got up and went out for a walk. I called him on the cell when I was ready to leave.

Of course, once they got back to their room after some fabulous coq au vin, perhaps, and an aged Merlot, he'd forget about how bored he'd been. Her perfect body would be clad in French underwear from a Parisian boutique that only the cognoscente knew about. It would be lime green or sea foam, and he'd lie in bed watching her undress, as if a present was being unwrapped for him. They'd make love and then maybe go out on the balcony and in the darkness watch the twinkling lights of the Bateaux-Mouches carrying tourists along the Seine.

I refused to think about him making love to her, especially when I was still sleeping in his bed. It didn't help that I dreamed about them. And it didn't help when I woke up in the middle of the night to go to the bathroom, only to kick something small and light that skidded across the hardwood floor. I turned on a light and walked over to see something gold and glittery. I lifted it up, and held it to the light, trying to focus my eyes. It looked like a child's necklace, and then I realized that no, it was an ankle bracelet with tiny pearls and diamonds. Engraved on a small gold plate in the middle was the word Bridget. I turned it over. The other side said, Chris.

Just before my fund–raiser, Jack Reilly called me. He was the last one I expected to hear from after the story ran.

"Your column got to me. Even I have a heart."

He said he wanted to send me a check for the event. I felt uncomfortable taking money from him, so I told him I was in the middle of something and that I'd call him back. Then I went to discuss it with Marty.

"As long as he isn't writing the check to you," he said with a smirk. I called Reilly back and told him he could mail me the check and gave him the name of the group to make it out to.

"I'm going down to St. Croix. I wanted to thank you for being the driving force behind changing my life."

"Jesus, Jack, you're something else." My article had no doubt sicced the D.A. on him, and now he was thanking me?

"I admire you," he said. "I really do. You've got your head on straight."

If he only knew. "Well, it's not on straight," I said. "It just looks that way compared to the posture of some of the people who I write about."

"Well, I hope we can have dinner when I'm back," he said. I didn't say anything.

What Men Want

★ ★ ★

Ellen was heading up to the Adirondacks to see Moose and she invited me along. I was prepared to protest. I'd be the third wheel, I was about to say. I'd get in the way. But I really wanted to go. We hadn't been together in so long, and I had been working so hard without a break. Just a few days out of the city would help me clear my head. I'd see how things went. I could always go off sight-seeing on my own for a few hours, if they wanted time to themselves.

There was also something particularly inviting about going to a place that was bitingly cold. It was a test of you against nature. And of course, I would be getting away from Chris's apartment. Somewhere in my bitter musings, I decided that until I got board approval for my co-op, I wasn't budging. If that inconvenienced him, it was too bad. He could wait it out at Bridget's place.

Ellen and I flew to Albany and then boarded a small commuter plane to Lake Placid. Moose met us at the airport in a pickup. Next to him, on the passenger seat, was a black-and-white Border collie. Her name was Sadie. Moose told her to jump into the back seat. She looked at us suspiciously for a moment, but then complied.

"How old is she?" I asked.

"Twelve," Moose said, shaking his head slightly. "She's getting up there." Sadie looked over at him lovingly, and then settled down on the blanket on the back seat and went to sleep.

He drove us to his house. When he opened the door, unlocked, it was as appealing as Ellen had described it.

"You'll always have a fallback career as a designer," I said, looking around at the spacious layout of the log cabin with the giant fireplace in the middle of the living room and all the bright colors of upholstery fabric on the rustic furniture, artfully arranged. "This should be photographed for a home-design magazine."

"It was," Moose said, clearly nonchalant by the whole thing. "The wife of a college buddy of mine was up here with him and she's an editor at *House & Home*. A crew came up and moved things around a little, and then took pictures."

"Did you get offers to buy it?"

"Oh sure," he said. "That always happens."

I got the tour of the kitchen—pine cabinets and concrete counters that he poured himself, and a wooden floor made of some type of barn siding. There was a large round dining table in the center of the room that, of course, he had made as well. Moose showed me a small sleeping loft, just above the living room, where there was a queen-size mattress covered with red flannel sheets and a down comforter. There was a skylight above it. During the day the room was filled with sun. At night there would be a view of the stars.

"And here I thought that you were some kind of hermit living in an outhouse-size place when Chris first told me about you," I said.

He smiled. "A little money goes a long way up here, especially if you can do the work yourself."

While he didn't have a regular job, Moose did carpentry work to earn money, and also wrote for various outdoor magazines. In the summer, he worked as a tour guide, and also had a small business making custom fly-fishing rods.

He obviously had a talent (the carpentry gene?). Could anyone just learn those skills or did you need to be wired to know how to build things and understand the laws of physics? What seems logical and natural to someone adept at using their hands is incomprehensible to me. I didn't share that with Moose, but I'm sure that he already knew it.

After coffee and sandwiches, we got into his truck with Sadie and he showed us the area. We drove down the main street of town that looked like a set design out of the forties. Then we drove to Lake Placid, sometimes dubbed Lake Plastic because the shops and restaurants are upscale—and so are the prices of real estate. I couldn't resist buying a pair of white furry Eskimo boots. Moose looked at me as if I was out of mind paying what I did. Of course, he could probably make a similar pair, except these, to my great relief, were made of fake fur. One less animal to slaughter.

I didn't discuss that with Moose. The more time I spent with him and Ellen, the more I began to think that he had it right. But did that mean that everyone should follow in his footsteps and give up city life for the wilderness? I didn't know if I could survive up here. I wondered about Ellen.

We walked halfway around Mirror Lake before going back to Moose's for dinner. After pasta with homemade marinara sauce, salad, bread and wine, he made a fire and we sat watching it.

"How's Chris?" Moose asked.

"Sore subject," Ellen said.

"He's in Paris with Bridget, the model for Model Thin, the diet drink he's writing about," I said.

He looked at me, surprised, and shook his head. "I don't give that long."

"Why do you say that?"

"He's sort of commitment phobic."

"What do you mean?"

"He dated a lot of girls in college, but he never seemed to stay with them for very long."

"Why do you think that was?"

"His parents were never any role models when it came to stability," he said. "They divorced and moved around a lot, never finding the right people to share their lives with."

"We were together for over a year."

"So what about you?" Ellen asked. "Didn't you have some kind of celebrity relationship?" I couldn't believe that she'd just asked him outright. I didn't add that we had the picture of him and Kelly Cartwright.

"For a while," he said.

"What happened?" Ellen asked.

"She went back to Hollywood to make another film."

"Did she break your heart?"

Moose looked at Ellen as though he was trying to figure out how much his answer meant to her. He shook his head.

"It was a fling—anyway, women usually give up on me," he said. "They don't think of this place as an antidote to civilization the way I do. For me, it's home, and I'm not going anyplace else."

"Not even New York?" I said in exaggerated disbelief.

"Not likely."

I smiled at Moose. He was a misfit, in a good way. He didn't fit in with the people that I knew and lived among, but he was an original. Moose knew himself and his needs. And he was principled. That alone would make him appeal to Ellen. If only she could figure out a way to make their relationship work geographically.

I got up and walked to the loft to go to sleep. The cold country air and the long walk had knocked me out and I pulled the down comforter around me. I heard Ellen and Moose talking softly by the fire and then as I was dozing off I noticed that the light was out and that they had gone to sleep. I envied the fact that they had each other to hold.

The calm and the cold helped me sleep deeper than I had in a long time. I woke at ten-thirty and then got up only out of guilt. Ellen and Moose had been up for hours. There were eggs and pancakes on the stove and they had gotten the newspapers. We all sat in front of the fire reading. Both of us wanted to spend an extra day, but with the fund-raiser coming up, we couldn't afford to be out of town. Ellen asked Moose if he would come in for it and he shook his head.

"Black-tie? I don't think so," he said. "You can tell me about it though." I could see that Ellen was disappointed, but she understood.

"I don't blame you," she said. "I hate black-tie functions too, and if this wasn't our shindig, I'd write a check instead of showing up." I told him about Slaid Warren's approach and that seemed to make sense to him.

"I know his stuff. I started reading it after I met him on an Outward Bound trip."

"Outward Bound?" I said. "I didn't know he was such an adventurer, but it doesn't surprise me."

"It started out as a travel article he was going to write. But then he really got into it. In fact, I don't even think that he ever wrote the piece. He just decided that trip was something that he wanted to do for himself."

"He's always testing," I said, still resentful over his horning in on our idea.

"Yeah, maybe when you grow up with a single parent, that's what you do," Moose said.

"What do you mean?"

"His dad was killed in Vietnam," Moose said. I didn't know.

"I wonder why that never came out?"

"Why would it? You live your life and you move on."

So I learned something new about my rival. Growing up in a single-parent household had to have made him more sensitive to suffering than those who grew up with the security of having two adults around. Despite the hardship, he had obviously done all right for himself.

We flew back to New York Sunday evening, going over the weekend together.

"He's got an enviable life," I said.

Ellen nodded. "Still, how could anyone he lived with survive up there full-time?"

"Well, you can't if you have to be on camera," I said, "but do you think that you're going to spend your life on the air doing consumer investigations? At some point you may just want to exchange the world of television for the world of nature—with the best outdoor guide that you could find."

"Eventually, maybe," she said. "But right now…"

The employment opportunities in one of the coldest and remotest places in the country were obviously limited. In fact, the population of Saranac Lake was just over five thousand, about the same size as my high school.

"Well, maybe you can get into furniture building, or designing log cabins," I said. "Or if all else fails, you could shovel snow."

"Well, I do shovel every day," Ellen said, "but it's not exactly pure white snow."

So we got lost in our separate worlds again once we were back in Manhattan. I was working on a new column about efforts to control New York City noise levels. After work I took the bus up Madison Avenue to a designer resale store to look for something to wear to our gala. The store was a treasure trove of cast-off designer gowns that society types turned in after just one wearing because they didn't want to be seen in the same outfit twice. The shop also sold shoes that had been worn for photo shoots but then couldn't be returned to the manufacturer and sold as new.

As it turned out, I did better than finding something gently used. I picked out a midnight-blue satin gown that still had the tags on it. It had spaghetti straps and a low-cut back. I found high-heeled silk sandals to go with it in a shoe store up the street.

I'm not usually one to brag, but the day of the event, things came together exactly the way I had hoped. I had had a haircut three weeks before, just enough time for it to grow the tiny bit it always needs to fall in the way I like. My hair color—just a notch lighter than usual—was warm, not brassy, and the new foundation and silver eyeshadow brought out my eyes and my pale complexion.

The event was going to begin at seven, and I met Ellen there at five to make sure that the caterer had brought all the food and that the bar was stocked. The wait staff were all dressed in white and when the guests started arriving, Ellen and I were at the door to welcome them. We rolled out a red carpet, and TV cameras were there along with the print media to record the arrival of every visitor.

It costs money to make money and while we had donations of food, wine and flowers, we spent on staff and rental of the tent, dishes and silverware. We showed a video spelling out the seriousness of the problem and then had speakers talking about what could be done to help the homeless, particularly children, if the city had adequate funds. Ellen and I circulated for most of the night, meeting people and greeting others whom we knew. We didn't know for sure how much money we had taken in, but we guessed that we had at least met more than seventy percent of our goals.

Marty was there, representing the paper, and for once he looked relaxed. I had never met his wife before, so I sat and chatted with her about the world of newspapers, which she left when their son was two.

"Do you miss it?" I asked her.

"Sometimes," she said. "But then when I hear what Marty went through during the day I'm glad I'm doing something else," she said. Something else turned out to be writing a novel about the newspaper business.

"That's one way to settle old scores," I said jokingly.

I excused myself to go the ladies' room, but as I was approaching the door, I felt a hand on my arm.

"Terrific dress," he whispered. I pivoted to find myself face-to-face with Slaid Warren.

"Oh," I said, unable to hide my surprise. "What are you doing here?"

"The same thing as everyone else," he said. I looked at him in his black tux with a black tuxedo shirt under it.

"Nice look," I said, gesturing toward his outfit.

"I thought so myself," he said, all modesty.

I smirked and he laughed.

"You're so gullible, George."

"So how's *your* event coming along?" I asked.

"It's really amazing. We started a Web site for people to visit to contribute ideas and tell us about the dinners they're planning." He shook his head. "You wouldn't believe the things they're cooking up."

"It was a brilliant idea," I said in all honesty.

"I thought so too. Unfortunately I can't take the credit for it."

"Who thought of it?"

Slaid scratched his head. "It's kind of a long story," he said. "Do you want to go someplace and have a drink?"

The evening was winding down and I was almost ready to head home anyway. Ellen said she'd hang around along with the interns from her office and supervise the cleanup crew. "Get out of here," she said, making sure she let me know that she saw Slaid. I picked up the Judith Leiber bag that I'd borrowed from her and I waved to Slaid. A few minutes later we were heading down Park Avenue.

"I just want you to know that I can't walk too far in these heels," I said.

"I'll carry you if you want," he said, straight-faced.

"You may have to," I said. He picked me up for a moment, and then put me down.

"Maybe a cab's not a bad idea," he said.

Chapter Nineteen

If you can stay awake until one or two in the morning, and you're out walking in Manhattan while the rest of the city sleeps, the city belongs to you. We stopped at my apartment and I traded my silk gown for a shirt, jeans and flat boots, and then we walked over three miles from Murray Hill down to Soho, talking about everything except newspapers.

Slaid talked about his father, an army captain whose jeep was blown up when he drove over a mine in Vietnam. He paused for a minute. "His tour was just about over," he said. "He was short—a week away from coming home." His mother had letters from him that he had written over the previous month talking about all the things that they would do together when he was back. They planned to go up to Cape Cod and rent a house, he said. Eventually, his father hoped to go into business for himself as a builder. Slaid stared off into the distance.

"In thirty seconds, three lives were blown apart." We talked about the ongoing problem of land mines that are hidden in the ground long after a war is over and the reasons for starting it are all but forgotten. We ended up in an all-night bar that he knew about because the owner was a former district attorney who got fed up with his job and traded his business suits for jeans and black T-shirts.

"So who gave birth to the idea of having small dinners to raise money for the homeless?" I asked him.

"My grandmother."

I raised an eyebrow.

"I swear. She was talking about a book group that she's in and how word of a good book spread from one branch of the group to another during small dinners that they held every other month at the members' houses."

"And that gave you the idea for the fund-raising dinners?"

"Well, I figured that if the grass-roots approach worked for spreading the word about a book, why shouldn't it work for getting people together to do good for the city?"

I nodded.

"And one more thing," he said.

"What's that?"

"I knew it would get your attention."

"So we're back to competing," I said as a statement rather than a question.

"No," he said, putting some money down on the table to pay the check. "Something else. But I guess the job is blindsiding you."

When we got back to the apartment, it was almost four. Slaid came up to see where I lived, or where I used to live, but I didn't get into that with him. I suppose that he noticed the plaques of advertising awards Chris had won that were on one of the bookshelves, but he didn't ask about them and I didn't explain.

He made himself comfortable on the couch with his feet propped up on the ottoman. I went into the kitchen and made us hot tea. I was sure that in the short time that I waited for the water to boil, he had examined the bookshelves and the overall apartment and gathered that I lived with someone, probably surmising that things were on the skids, otherwise why would I have invited him up?

I brought two mugs over to the coffee table and sat down next to him. It wasn't as though I planned to do anything more than talk, but before I knew it, I was leaning my head back on the couch and his mouth was over mine.

"Look—" I said, starting to protest, although I wasn't sure why. He had soft lips, full lips, and soon they were pressing against mine harder and harder and I was kissing him back with more passion and heat than I expected. He unbuttoned the top button of my blouse, and then the one beneath it, and then the one beneath that, and slowly, I reached around and pulled down the shoulders of his tuxedo jacket, making it easy for him to slide out of it. His shirt came off next, tossed onto the floor. His body was the way I imagined it, smooth, muscular, the sinewy build of a swimmer, not someone who pumps iron. A moment later, I was lying back on the couch, and Slaid was leaning over me. I don't remember what I was saying, or wasn't, but suddenly my attention went from his lips and the feel of his fingers running through my hair to the sound of a key slipping into the lock of the door. The two of us turned our heads simultaneously, and I pulled away, ready to jump up, convinced that someone was trying to break in. It was so late and I was so tired that I couldn't recall if I had double locked the door or not. At that moment, the door flew open.

Chris walked in and dropped his suitcase, staring at us for a minute without saying anything. There was a confused look on his face, as if he had entered the wrong apartment and couldn't figure out what was happening.

"What the hell is going on?" he asked finally. I pulled my blouse up over me.

"What are you doing here?" I demanded. "You were supposed to be in Paris."

"I *was* in Paris. I just got back."

"You could have called." I didn't know what else to say.

"I guess you forgot that this is my apartment." He looked at Slaid who sat there, silently, not knowing what to make of what was happening.

"Who the fuck are you?" Chris said.

"And who the fuck are you?" Slaid said back.

"Jenny's former boyfriend," Chris said, putting the emphasis on "former" as though what he had just witnessed was what caused the relationship to recede into the past tense.

"Where's your model girlfriend?" I asked him, beginning to steam at the nerve of him coming back in the middle of the night without first calling. He had another relationship, why the hell did he think that I was just sitting around pining for him without having a life of my own.

"She went to her place," he said flatly. He looked around and raked his fingers through his hair, obviously not knowing what to do now that he had arrived with his suitcase. Clearly, things with Bridget hadn't gone the way he expected.

"I see," I said coolly, even though I didn't.

Slaid stood up, putting his shirt back on and quickly buttoning it up. He didn't bother to tuck it in. He looked over at me.

"Do you want me to stay?" he said, moving closer to me.

I shook my head. "No, thanks, it's okay."

He grabbed his jacket and slung it over his shoulder. He gave Chris one last cool glance before he turned back to me. "I'm sorry, Jen," he said softly, giving me a wistful look. "I'll call you later." I watched him close the door behind him and then turned to look at Chris.

"So what's going on?" I said. Chris looked ready to cry.

"The fuckin' plane was diverted to London on the way back because of a bomb threat. I haven't slept in twenty-four goddamn hours, and now I come back to my own place and find you screwing on the couch with some jerk you probably just met."

"First of all, we weren't screwing on the couch," I said. "And second of all, who he is or isn't is none of your business." I stood up and realized that I had never buttoned my blouse, even though I had hastily pulled it around me. I closed the middle button, and then headed for the bathroom as he opened the refrigerator door and grabbed a soda.

"In the meantime," I said, turning back to him, "I'm dead tired and don't want to be talking about any of this right now, so why don't you just sleep on the couch. We can deal with this tomorrow." With that, I went into the bathroom to wash off my makeup. Then without looking back into the living room, I went into the bedroom and got into bed. I slept fitfully for most of the next day, waking every few hours, not sure whether it was day or night. When I finally got out of bed, it was almost three in the afternoon. Chris was gone, and so was his suitcase.

One day went by and then another as if life was nothing more than a revolving door between office and home. Chris didn't call, and neither did Slaid. Had Chris gone back to Bridget? Was he just marking time until he called and wanted to move back into his apartment? I went through every possible scenario. I did the same thing with Slaid, trying to imagine whether he had merely thrown up his hands and assumed that I was back with Chris or whether he'd just decided to move on after his aborted opportunity.

Why is it always easier to see what's going on in everyone else's life, but when it comes to your own, everything is blurred and out of focus? To distract myself, I went to a knitting store and spent over a hundred dollars on wool for a Fair Isle cardigan that I was ready to give up on when I saw how complicated it would be to knit. I cast on stitches for the left arm, and then stuck the needles with two rows of knitting into the magazine rack. I went out to eat, but got mad at myself for having a monstrously large portion of meat loaf with gravy, and mashed potatoes, followed by apple pie with vanilla ice cream.

Another day I went shopping, and, of course, everything that I tried on was tight. Was it because I had probably gained five pounds or merely because *every* designer was now making their clothes one size smaller?

Finally I decided that the best place to lose myself was the gym. After an hour-long workout, I went for a massage. The therapist seemed to intuit just where my stress points were and using a combination of Swedish massage and shiatsu, she stroked, poked, pulled and pushed until my body turned into what felt like a loaf of freshly kneaded dough. Human contact, and pampering without the strings attached. It was a welcome alternative to complicated relationships. To pamper my kink-free body even further, all I had for dinner was a fruit smoothie from Jamba Juice. I came home, watched a mindless show on TV and then went to sleep.

Exactly ten days after I had seen Chris, I was at work, struggling to come up with a riveting lead for a column on a judge in landlord-tenant court when the phone rang.

"Hi," Chris said.

There was silence for a few seconds. I took a deep breath. "Hi."

"Jen, look, I'm sorry that I just barged in on you," he said. "I…I…" He seemed at a loss for words. "Can we just meet for dinner?"

"Okay…where."

"Whatever," he said, true to form. "What are you in the mood for?"

"Let's meet for Chinese at seven," I said. He named

a Chinese restaurant in Times Square. The food was good and came before you had a chance to close the menu. He could say what he had to and then I'd be on my way. It was clear that the living arrangements would have to be discussed. He didn't know yet about the co-op that I hoped to buy, and I'd let him know what the timetable would be. Like two people going through a divorce, we'd have to decide who'd get what articles of furniture since we had purchased several pieces, including our new Pottery Barn sofa, together.

I got there first, and sat down on the bench in the front, watching customers go in and out, while staring at the brown, glazed Peking ducks that were hanging upside down near the kitchen. I vowed never to have another serving of duck. The poor pathetic creatures. What did they do to deserve that? As I was lost in thought, Chris came up to me, startling me by planting a kiss on my cheek.

"Hi," he said. "Sorry I'm late."

I didn't say anything. The hostess showed us to a table, and a moment later, we were staring at menus that listed what seemed like a hundred different dishes.

"So how are things?" I asked after the waitress had taken our orders. I felt awkward and uncomfortable, while retreating behind a protective cloak so that he couldn't hurt me anymore. Would we ever again be able to laugh together and share things the way we used to? I pulled my sweater around my shoulders. Only then did I realize that it was the cashmere cardigan that he had gotten me for Christmas.

He looked at me intently, narrowing his eyes. "How are things? Terrible," he said. I really didn't want to hear the details of what was going wrong in his life, so I just sat there without encouraging him to explain.

"Look, Jen, I made a really big mistake," he said. "I guess the idea of getting involved with this gorgeous model who liked me really blindsided me to who she was and what I was giving up.

"She's like some fifteen-year-old princess who's probably going to have a nervous breakdown in the next five years," he said, shaking his head. "I had no idea what that whole world was like, but believe me, it's not something that anybody with a brain would want to get into."

"Well, I'm sorry things didn't work out for you," I said. He looked back at me, startled.

"Jen, I want to get back together," Chris said, as if he had to make it clearer because I wasn't getting the message. "I want to just forget about the last few weeks and pick up the life that we had. All I kept thinking about in Paris was that I had given up something real for a stupid fling."

Was the word *fling* part of the popular lexicon now? I guess he had been talking to Moose, I thought as the waitress brought our meals.

"I don't know," I said finally. "I can't just forget about what happened and get over it."

"Look, I know," Chris said. "But can we try to, maybe slowly, start things up again? If you want I'll stay with one of the art directors in my office. A couple of them have big apartments. I know they'd put me up. We can date, see how thing go."

I looked back at him, not sure what to say.

"Maybe," I said, scratching the side of my face as though I had suddenly gotten an itchy hive. "Maybe."

We sat through the rest of the meal sharing a strained silence, like two people on an awkward first date. I know that he wanted to tell me more about his trip, but I didn't ask him. I didn't want to know. There was no way to clear the air if you didn't discuss what happened, but I didn't have it in me to ask him, and he knew that I wasn't ready to hear. I had gone over this scenario again and again in my head. Now it was a reality, but I wasn't prepared.

We left the restaurant, and I realized that I had forgotten to tell Chris that I was in the process of buying a studio apartment. We hadn't even gotten to that point. Now it was almost irrelevant.

Chapter Twenty

It came as no surprise that the grand jury indicted Jack Reilly on federal bribery charges. And it came as no surprise that three people in the Mayor's Office of Film, Theatre and Broadcasting were indicted along with him. Thanks to his money and connections, I had no doubt that Reilly's ass would probably be saved. After all, he was being represented by a team of the country's top criminal lawyers who had a cadre of eager law students with time and energy to help them unearth every smidgen of evidence they could find to show that Reilly was an upstanding member of the film world who brought riches to every city he filmed in and often entertained friends from different professions without any ulterior motives.

Marilyn had a few skeletons in her closet—she had been arrested for shoplifting twenty years earlier, I knew—and they would dig up anything that they could to malign her and her character. Reilly would claim to have no awareness that people in his office were putting together bogus bills. The staff would be disbanded, and he would distance himself from all of them.

I was sure that he would work out a deal with the government that would reduce, if not eliminate, the chances of him doing any prison time. What I wasn't sure about was whether you could be put under house arrest if you'd recently switched your residence to St. Croix from Los Angeles. It was almost a joke to think of him being imprisoned in a Caribbean villa with a swimming pool and tennis courts and his own private beach, welcoming the girlfriend of the hour to console him until his sentence was served.

The indictment triggered Slaid to write a column about getting away with murder if you had enough money to buy the services of the best defense lawyers in the country. He named case after case where liars, cheats and murderers went free while those whose guilt was uncertain, at best, but had no means to hire decent lawyers, were doomed to long prison terms.

"Nice job," I said.

"But?"

"But nothing."

It was almost two weeks since I had seen Slaid. I knew that he had been waiting for me to call.

"I'm disappointed," he said. "I was hoping to hear that fighting spirit again."

"I feel like all our work is for nothing. They're out of jail with a slap on the wrist, thinking of the next way to pull one over on honest jerks like us."

"Well, we haven't run out of bad guys," he said. "Don't act as though there's no more dirt for you to sweep up."

"Um, I suppose."

"So what happened to your boyfriend?" he said, changing the subject.

No easy answer to that. Chris had come over a few nights after we had dinner. We rented a movie and ordered take-out Chinese food. I had my guard up, and was consumed with wondering whether I could ever trust him again and feel the closeness that we once had. I guess he sensed that because aside from sitting close to me on the couch, and at one point leaning over to kiss my neck, he didn't ask to stay over and he left at eleven.

"We're in transition," I said to Slaid.

"Transition? Isn't that some stage of childbirth, or something?"

"I wouldn't know."

"But it doesn't mean we can't have dinner, right?"

I took a deep breath. "No, I guess not."

"Okay then," he said, "I'll pick you up tomorrow at seven."

★ ★ ★

We were going to head down to Soho to have dinner at the Mercer Kitchen. Slaid lived nearby, and told me that it was one of his favorite restaurants.

Then I got the call from Ellen.

"You won't believe where I am," she said, obviously upset.

"I give up."

"At New York Hospital. I slipped on the ice on the way out of the studio and fractured my ankle."

"What?"

"I work out every goddamn day of my life. I can't believe this."

It turned out that it was just a freak accident, but she'd be in an air cast that she had to wear for a month.

"I was supposed to go visit Moose this weekend. Now I'm stuck here for the duration."

"Did you tell him?"

"No."

"Why not?"

"I don't know," Ellen said. "You know how much he hates the city…."

"Well, you have to let him know."

"I will," she said.

"I'll be there as soon as I can. I'll take you home."

I hung up and got into a cab. It was only then that I realized that I was supposed to meet Slaid in fifteen minutes. I phoned him and explained.

"I'll meet you at the emergency room," Slaid said. "After we take her home we can get some dinner nearby." He joined me as I waited, over an hour, for Ellen. While we waited, Slaid took the crutches the nurse had brought for Ellen and hobbled around the room, like a kid who has to play with a new toy put in front of him.

"They're about two feet too small for you," I said, amused by his performance.

"To the untrained eye, yes," he said. Then he lifted his knees as though he were doing an ab exercise, and used them to support him as he did a handstand. A nurse walked by and shook her head.

"This isn't a circus," she said snappishly. "Would you mind sitting down?"

"Yeah, sure," he said, flipping himself down on the bench. He turned to me and whispered, "They're such a humorless bunch."

"That tends to happen after you work around the clock and don't sleep for two days."

"You should know," he said, obviously referring to the column I wrote on exhaustion in the E.R. after the son of a prominent politician died because his fever and pain were misdiagnosed by a sleep-deprived intern.

"And I remember your call. I couldn't imagine why a columnist at the *Trib* whom I'd never met would call and tell me that I didn't know the half of it."

"I was dating a doctor, at the time. And I wanted to do the story, but she swore that if I did it would come back to haunt her. Everyone knew she was seeing me, so I held off. I figured I'd write it when her rotation changed, but you broke the back of it, so I figured I'd go on to something else."

"So if I broke the back of it, why did you bother to call?"

He shrugged. "I kind of studied your picture.... You were cute."

Once she got home, Ellen called Moose and told him what happened. He asked her how she felt, and aside from saying that she was depressed to be on crutches, she said she was fine. They hung up without discussing when they would see each other again. Eight hours later, when there was a knock on her door, and she hobbled to answer it, needless to say she was surprised to see Moose standing there along with Sadie.

"She's great at retrieving things," Moose said. "That's why I brought her." Never mind that every couch and chair would soon have a film of white dog hair, Ellen was thrilled to have their company.

"You didn't have to do this," Ellen told him.

"I know," he said. Moose said he'd stay in town as long as she wanted company. He even offered to take her back with him so that he could take care of her up at his house.

"The scenery's a lot prettier. Why don't you come back with me?"

"I have to work," Ellen said unconvincingly.

"You must get some kind of disability," he tried.

She looked at him for a long minute. "Are you sure you want me?" He picked her up, and carried her to the door.

Ellen spent one week at Moose's house and then another. She called often to give me updates. He was going to the store to buy food, but she did the cooking, hobbling around the kitchen in her boot, she said. She also spent time reading books, something she rarely had time to do when she was in the city. She called me one morning to tell me that she had been looking through his bookshelf and had found a poetry anthology. Inside the cover there was a folded piece of paper.

"He wrote a poem after his dog died," she said. "It was so touching that I started to cry."

I sat there at my desk, nodding. "I'd fall in love with a guy like that too." I said, knowing what she was thinking.

"The funny thing is," said Ellen, her voice breaking with emotion, "I looked over at Sadie. She got up and came right over and sat down next to me. We've become really good friends over the past two weeks. I know she understood." When Moose came home, she asked him about the poem, she said.

"Moose said that he'd been pretty close to the dog

and when it died he felt like he'd lost a member of his family."

"He's a lovely guy, Ellen," I said, as if it was my mission to make her know that. She didn't answer. Finally, I asked her when she was coming back.

"In a week."

"Great," I said.

She didn't say anything.

I was on my way out of the building on the way to work when the doorman stopped me.

"You got flowers," he said, pointing to an arrangement of roses and greenery sitting in a glass vase. I walked over and opened the tiny envelope that was pinned to the stem of a rose:

Dinner tonight? Chris

I slid the note back in the envelope and told the doorman to hold them for me until I got home. I was still living in Chris's apartment because I didn't close on mine and he was staying with someone from his agency, as if he had been disenfranchised.

We'd lived together for an entire year, but why did I feel nervous now about seeing him again? Was his relationship with Bridget always going to sit in the room like an elephant that I couldn't forget?

I got on a Limited bus, pushing my way to the back so that I could find a sliver of room where I could hold on. I thought about where we should have dinner. We always loved going down to the Meatpacking District to a steak restaurant called Frank's, on Tenth Avenue and Fifteenth Street. The wide streets, once deserted after business hours, were now bustling with diners and shoppers who frequented boutiques with very uptown prices. When I got to my desk, I sent Chris an e-mail:

Pretty flowers. Thanks. There's a pub party for our music critic's new book on the rock mystique. Promised I'd go. It's at the Hard Rock Café. Want to meet me there? Then dinner at Periyali's? He messaged me back in minutes.

Cool, C

It wasn't one of the days when I had to file. In fact, it was a slow day, when I was just putting together some ideas for future stories and making a string of phone calls. I got out of work earlier than expected, so I stopped at the apartment to change into something more interesting before heading to the Hard Rock on West Fifty-seventh Street. I exchanged my plain brown gabardine slacks for black leather pants. I added a black cashmere sweater, and was pretty happy with the look. Stylish, but not screaming for attention. It briefly crossed my mind that someone like Bridget might be there—it was a party, after all, but then no, I remembered that Ethan was more of a nerdy, intellectual reporter, not a flashy rock type, even though he wrote about the scene.

I got to the party a few minutes before I was supposed to meet Chris. It would give me time to talk to Ethan, congratulate him and spend the requisite amount of time before we could leave and go eat. As I expected, the music was loud and pounding, the perfect setting.

Book parties don't sell books, still authors enjoy celebrating the birth of their books, and book parties are a way of marking the event. No surprise that everyone in the music scene showed up, ranging from rock performers to people from record labels, to those in production and publishing.

"Ethan," I said when I saw him near the door. "Congratulations, I can't wait to read it."

"I hate the cover," he whispered to me. "Can you believe how dull it is for a book on rock music?"

"It's moody and evocative," I said, reaching. "Your name alone will sell it whether it has a cover or not." He smiled and patted me on the back and then was pulled away by one of the drama critics.

I headed for the bar and ordered a glass of white wine, when a voice over my shoulder whispered, "We have to stop meeting like this."

I turned and was face-to-face with Slaid.

"Oh," I said, startled. "How do you know Ethan?"

"Ethan who?"

I raised an eyebrow. "The author?"

"Oh, *that* Ethan. He's my upstairs neighbor. I haven't paid for a CD since I met him—great neighbor." He paused and looked at me.

"So how are you doing?" he said, turning serious.

"Fine," I said, looking back at him levelly.

"Got the boyfriend thing worked out?"

How did I answer that one? I shrugged.

"Well, why don't we say goodbye to Ethan and go get—"

"Jen, I was looking for you," Chris said, suddenly behind me, putting his hands on my shoulders. He looked at Slaid with a trace of annoyance. "Ready to go?" he said, kissing the side of my face.

"Yes," I said, stepping down from the bar stool. "I'll see you," I said to Slaid. He curled the tips of his fingertips and waved.

Chris didn't ask about Slaid, or even mention him again, but I sensed that just seeing him made him feel more proprietary about me. He slipped his hand around my waist and held me close to him as we walked down Fifty-seventh Street looking for a cab to take us to Periyali, a Greek restaurant on West Twentieth Street. *Periyali* is a Greek word that means seashore, or coastline, and it was easy to transport myself into a taverna by the sea. The walls were white plaster with dark wooden beams across the ceiling, white cotton tenting between them that could make you feel as though you're staring at the giant sail of a boat. Photographs of Patmos, with its white box-like houses bathed in the Aegean sun were on the walls, framed in dark, handsome wood that matched the ceiling beams and floorboards.

Patmos was the kind of place that I always thought about escaping to with Chris. We would hike, or ride donkeys to the monastery on the top and go swimming in the late afternoon before we sat at an outdoor taverna and had fish with tomato salad and feta cheese. But we never found the time to go. Or maybe we just never really wanted to, because the only places that we went were movies or plays, or weekend drives to the Hamptons and Connecticut or the Pennsylvania Dutch country, sending everyone postcards from Intercourse, PA.

We studied the menu and ordered salads, moussaka, grilled fish and a bottle of retsina. Even though I knew that he was still working on the account, Chris carefully avoided any talk of Model Thin or Bridget. Of course, I'd seen one print ad and a TV commercial. I must say, the ad looked convincing. They shot her walking along a beach in a bikini wearing a big straw hat. In her hand is a can of Model Thin. A smiling Bridget walks along the water, sipping happily, and finally turns to the camera and smiles.

"How do I stay model thin?" She holds up the can. In another commercial she's sitting at a beachside bar with a thatched roof, drinking what looks like a piña colada, but, of course, it's a tall-stemmed glass filled with Model Thin. She turns to the camera, which slowly pans up and down her body.

"It's just me and Model Thin," she says. "I have nothing to hide."

I didn't discuss the commercials with Chris. What was the point? And in our one brief telephone conversation about what happened between them, he told me that he thought of her now as an airhead who loved being the center of attention, and all that she thought about were her wardrobe and career. He mentioned the "blank stare" that she gave him when he started talking one night about jazz greats like John Coltrane and Chet Baker. I suppose it didn't help things when she told him that the last book she had read was, *The Sisterhood of the Traveling Pants.*

What he did tell me about were the ads that he started working on for a health-food chain that would be in direct competition with Whole Foods.

"Did you suggest that they call it Model Foods," I asked archly.

"That's right," he said, obviously emboldened by his third glass of retsina. "We'll use a perfect talking tomato in the ads," he said, gesturing dramatically. "Or a hot chili pepper." We laughed and suddenly he looked at me imploringly.

"Jen, can I move back in with you? I can't stay out of the apartment forever."

"Chris, I—"

"If you want we'll get engaged," he said, reaching over the table to take my hand. "I don't want to be with other women…we'll think about getting married," he said.

I pulled my hand back, holding the edge of the table. The last thing I ever expected to hear from Chris at this point was a proposal. Was this a last-ditch effort on his part to get us back together, or did he really think it through and want to marry me?

Do you really love me? I wanted to ask him, because now there was this gulf of the unsaid between us. Just because his fling didn't work out, did that mean our relationship was perfect enough to lead to marriage? But I didn't say all of that because at that moment, reflecting on the prospect of spending the rest of my life with him, I knew what my answer was.

"I can't," I said weakly.

"So we can just move back together…" he started. "We don't have to—"

"Chris, I bought an apartment." I realized now that I had never told him. How could I have, we had spent so little time talking. "The board approved the sale and I'm moving in at the end of the month." He looked as though he had been slapped.

"I'm sorry, Chris." I looked up and the waiter was standing next to us.

"Would you like to see the dessert menu?"

"No thanks," I said. "I'm really full."

What Men Want

We left the restaurant more like strangers than former lovers. Despite the wine, I felt that for the first
time I was seeing things clearly. I couldn't imagine
being married to Chris. I didn't love him. What we
had was comfortable. Convenient. Easy. But it wasn't
love. It took Model Thin to shape me up.

Chapter Twenty-One

The movers didn't arrive until after eleven, mumbling something about a truck that broke down. Then they had to compete for the service elevator with another company that was moving someone else out. By the time we got to my new apartment and all my belongings were carted up, it was after six o'clock in the evening.

I had forfeited my half of the Pottery Barn couch to Chris, along with the West Elm coffee table because I couldn't face the idea of trying to come up with acceptable terms for dividing them. I couldn't imagine what couples went through who had lived together for years and had a house filled with joint purchases, not to mention children and pets. At least there was no bitterness between us.

How could I ever forget the story that I heard

about a couple who was in the midst of an ugly divorce. Because the relationship had become so acrimonious, neither of them was willing to give the other their beloved dog. Instead, the poor creature was brought to a shelter and left for adoption.

Fortunately, Chris and I had never shared either pets or children and it was almost therapeutic to be forced to clean house. I ended up with a half-empty new apartment and it felt right to live in a raw, unfinished state, since it seemed to stand for the rest of my life. A queen-size mattress on a blond wood platform from Crate & Barrel sat in the L-shaped alcove, and a pine table and matching chairs from Ikea were outside the kitchen, defining a dining area. There wasn't much else in the room, except a desk with my computer and a leopard-print chair, but since I'd painted the apartment apple green, it felt fresh and happy to me.

I was sitting on the edge of my bed one day channel surfing when I came upon a commercial for Model Thin and it made me think of Chris. It had been almost a month since I had seen him. There was Bridget once again, this time standing on the side of a yacht, her hair blowing softly in the breeze. She was wearing a three-quarter-sleeve, black T-shirt with just a tiny black-and-white polka-dot bikini bottom accenting legs that were about eight feet long.

She smiled at the camera, and took a sip of the drink. "Find the new and better you, inside of you,"

she said. I smiled. Inadvertently, Chris and Bridget
had helped me script my life, no thanks to the drink
though. It took losing him to gain the recognition
of who and what I was and what I needed. It reminded me of the gym motto—"No pain, no gain."

My thirty-sixth birthday came and went unevent-
fully, despite the fact that I was thinking about it as
if it were some kind of middle-aged milestone.
Thirty-six sounded much more definitive than
thirty-four or thirty-five, and was edging up there toward forty. Still, I didn't feel any different the next
day. No gray hairs suddenly revealed themselves
along the part of my hair. No age lines were etched
into my skin around my eyes, beyond the ones that
were already there. What I did do was go to a hair
colorist recommended by the beauty editor at my
paper and for the first time, I had a mixture of high-
lights and lowlights so that I felt as though my hair
color accented my skin, like makeup, even when I
wasn't wearing any. Then I went to Saks and bought
myself a sleek navy blue silk nightgown. It wasn't to
impress anyone. I bought it because I liked it and it
made me feel sexy and womanly, even though these
days I was sleeping in the middle of the bed instead
of on one side and it wouldn't have mattered if the
nightgown were made of flannel, or was as tough as
horsehair.

FedEx dropped a package at my building on my
birthday. It was a pair of snowshoes from Ellen and

Moose and an invitation to come up to the house for a weekend. I called Ellen just after I was sitting down to dinner one night and saw her on TV. I usually did a double take. It's not that I should have been surprised. I knew when she was on. It was just that her TV persona was so different from the best friend that I knew in real life. As soon as she was off the air, I knew that I'd be able to reach her. She usually went back to her office and started by scrubbing off her heavy theatrical makeup.

"Thanks for the great gift," I said.

"It was the one thing that I knew you wouldn't have."

"I love them, and I accept your offer." Then I moved on to her. "So how are you?"

"Happy to be back working, but I'm looking forward to seeing Moose again in a couple of weeks. It was so great to take off all that time." Then she paused. "I really like him, actually love him," Ellen said matter-of-factly.

"Did he ask you to stay?"

"Well, he knew I wouldn't stay, but we talked about spending more time together. And I agreed to come up for holidays and all of August if he'd come down and see me."

"He agreed?"

"I think he realizes that if he's going to have a life with someone, he's got to give a little," she said. "I'm not about to give up my career—at least not at this point—but I also don't want to spend my life alone and never see him."

"So let me guess. The action reporter took action."

"Of course."

The plan was smart, it combined his love of the outdoors with Ellen's commitment to mentoring kids in need. She put together a group from an inner-city high school who, as part of a science project, would meet with Moose on a monthly basis at the school, and the rest of the time communicate by e-mail. He would put together an outdoor-survival course (Adirondack Survival?) and at the end of school the three kids who scored the highest got to get out of the city and, along with the science teacher, spend five days camping in the Adirondacks with Moose, applying what they had learned.

"He loved the idea," Ellen said. "I think he always wanted to do something with kids but didn't know how to get started."

While Moose got calls from schools periodically to come in and do workshops on nature, he was never able to find anything on a steady basis.

"The kids loved him. He has a better rapport with them than with their teachers." They were fascinated with the frontier clothes that he wore and told them that he had made them himself, not to mention the tepee that he put up on the front lawn of the schools so that the kids could play inside.

It was obvious to me that anyone who met Moose and talked to him for more than a minute about the outdoor world would see that he'd be a perfect teacher. It took Ellen to find a way for him to work with students without the requisite teaching credits.

As usual, Slaid Warren and I were keeping pace with each other and covering many of the same stories. Ever since I had seen him at the book party for our music critic, he had been uncharacteristically silent. One column of mine came out, and then another, and still, no phone calls.

Then, a week later, Slaid ran a column describing the plight of a man accused of robbery who was facing a long prison term because his attorney practically slept through the case. My column the next day went into the city's shortage of legal-aid lawyers. After that one, he didn't call me to offer praise, he called to ask me to have dinner.

"How about someplace French, snobby and obscenely expensive?" he said.

"Serious food?"

"Very," he said.

"That might work."

"Eight o'clock?"

"Perfect," I said.

We went to Le Bernardin. It opened in 1986 after Gilbert and Maguy Le Coze had made a name for themselves with their restaurant in Paris. Billed as French, formal and all about fish, it received four stars months after it opened, and again in 1995, just a year after the death of Gilbert. There was usually a wait to get a reservation. I didn't ask Slaid how he got the table, but I assumed that he'd probably offered his firstborn.

"Have you been here before?" I asked him as we were seated in a formal dining room with navy blue walls and honey-colored wooden chairs and banquettes.

"No," he said, "but *Gourmet* magazine said that if you can't close the deal here, you probably can't close it anywhere. That kind of stuck with me."

"Oh," I said, not sure how to take that. Was he about to hit me up for a donation to some new charity? I hoped not.

The sommelier brought the wine list and Slaid studied it briefly before asking for something white, from California. That was followed by blackened redfish tournedos, truffled Napa cabbage roll with goat's-milk yogurt sauce and a mushroom tart. Those were the appetizers. For the main course we had steamed striped bass and okra in a spicy pineapple-lime nage with coriander-jasmine rice and eggplant chutney and crispy Chinese spiced black bass in a Peking duck bouillon scented with maitake and enoki mushrooms.

"Same old, same old," I said as the food was brought to the table.

"They do these dishes in our cafeteria every day," he said, shaking his head in dismay. "It's so yesterday."

We didn't do a tremendous amount of talking as we ate. It seemed almost sacrilegious to divert our attention from the food. When it was time for dessert, I looked at the menu.

"I'll have the yuzu," I said, which was a lemon tart with ginger parfait topped with a thin caramel tuile.

"Kudzu? Jesus, don't order that, the damn vines start growing around your intestines…"

"Yuzu," I said.

He ordered the dark chocolate, cashew and caramel tart, put his fork into it and held out the fork to me.

"In case it's poison?"

"Are we always going to be battling this current of competition?" Slaid said, pulling back the fork teasingly as I was about to taste the dessert.

"Well, I doubt that we're going to forget that we're competitors," I said.

He shook his head up and down in agreement. "It does make it hard to relate like a normal couple who are open and honest with each—"

"Who share their secrets, their concerns and their work," I said, finishing his thought.

He nodded again. "Yeah, well, you're right. I thought maybe there was a chance, but—"

"But nothing," I said, finishing his thought again. "It was a marvelous dinner, truly memorable, especially tomorrow when I step on the scale. You were fun to be with and I really appreciate your generosity. I'm sure this dinner cost you a bundle."

"And how," he said, shaking his head in mock disbelief.

"Well, I guess I'd better head home," I said. "I've got to file tomorrow, and I hate to start a column when I'm sleep deprived."

"Understand," he said.

We walked out on West Fifty-first Street, and headed for the East Side.

"Maybe we should walk just a little, to help digest the meal," he said. We walked toward Fifth Avenue, toward the lights of Trump Tower. Slaid had his arm lightly on my shoulder, and we admired jewels in the windows of Harry Winston and Tiffany as we crisscrossed the streets.

We stopped when we got to the carriages of Central Park to part ways and head home.

"It would have been nice," he said, "if things had been different."

"Mmm, maybe some other place, some other time," I said. He kissed me lightly on the forehead, and headed to the subway to go downtown. I began walking toward the street where someone had just gotten out of a cab that pulled up. Then, just as suddenly, I turned around, putting my hands together in front of my mouth.

"Hey, Slaid," I yelled out. He stopped and turned

around to face me with a questioning look on his face. Slowly, it was replaced by an impish grin. I ran up to him, and then jumped up, pulling myself up on his shoulders. He grabbed my legs and walked forward, carrying me, piggyback, down along the street.

Also by Deborah Blumenthal…

Fat Chance

Fat Chance is the story of plus-size Maggie, also
known as America's Anti-Diet Sweetheart, who is
perfectly happy with who she is and the life she
leads. Until she gets a call from Hollywood's most
enticing bachelor, Mike Taylor. Bursting with wit,
insight and heart, this delicious novel reaches beyond
the story of Maggie O'Leary to every woman who has
tried to find fulfillment. *Fat Chance* is a lusciously
guilt-free pleasure that is good to the last page!

"*Fat Chance* is a modern Cinderella story…
and great fun!"
—Susan Issacs, author of *Long Time No See*

Are you getting it at least twice a month?

Here's how: Try RED DRESS INK books on for size & receive two FREE gifts!

Bombshell
by Lynda Curnyn

As Seen on TV
by Sarah Mlynowski

RDI04-TR